It Can Happen Here

IT CAN HAPPEN
HERE

A NOVEL LOOK BACKWARD

MAX J. SKIDMORE

Westphalia Press
An Imprint of the Policy Studies Organization
Washington, DC
2020

Westphalia Press
An imprint of Policy Studies Organization
1527 New Hampshire Ave., NW
Washington, D.C. 20036
info@ipsonet.org

ISBN: 978-1-941472-39-2

Cover and interior design by Jeffrey Barnes
jbarnesbook.design

Daniel Gutierrez-Sandoval, Executive Director
PSO and Westphalia Press

Updated material and comments on this edition
can be found at the Westphalia Press website:
www.westphaliapress.org

Dedicated with sincere gratitude

*To those saving the United States as
a constitutional republic*

President Joseph R. Biden, Jr.

Vice President Kamala Harris

The Democratic Party

TABLE OF CONTENTS

THE RATIONALE

No doubt historians will throw their collective efforts into analyses of the tumultuous years ending the fiasco of the recent, unlamented, administration and the beginning of Biden and Harris as president and vice president. In the spirit of the more the merrier, I am doing my part.

You, my family have asked for this, although you may have had no idea what you'd be getting. I've put it off for a while, but if I'm going to do it, I'd better get it done. I have not been especially close, but as you've said, I've been close enough to the action that perhaps there would be enough significance in what I've observed to leave a record for you and the rest of my family, especially the coming generations. Perhaps it might also be helpful to others too.

This isn't the memoir that you and others have asked me to do. Someday I may actually get around to it, but I think it is more important at this time that I leave all of you my thoughts on one of the most bizarre times in America's political history. My sketches may mirror, or they may contradict, those who have made it a profession to analyze the joys and terrors of American politics, but I have concluded that I owe it to you and all those close to me to contribute to the entire picture. Putting a personal stamp on it may make it more meaningful to my loved ones, so I'm not attempting a formal history here. I hope that doesn't invalidate my work and observations for others. Perhaps they can benefit from another perspective, even though it comes from an ancient, straight, white guy.

For a little background, I have lived in both India and Hong Kong, which have given me a broadened outlook. My travels have taken me many places, including each of the fifty states and every continent, including Antarctica. In America, I live in the Midwest where I was born and have lived much of my life off and on. I have lived in the North, where I earned a doctorate (Minnesota). I have lived and worked in the East, in Baltimore and the Washington, DC area, and in the Southwest. I have lived in the Deep South during the George Wallace days (the old Bad George Wallace, not the later somewhat better George Wallace), where I first had the experience (one that I do not recommend highly, although it worked out well), of having a gun pulled on me.

So here we go. This consists of material from The Journal , as I have, perhaps grandiosely, termed my notes. It demonstrates the truth of Sinclair Lewis's ironic title: *It Can't Happen Here.* In fact, as he was warning, it can happen here, indeed, and briefly (although not briefly enough), it did.

Instead of presenting it in regular journal style, I have excerpted the material, and arranged it into chapters. I must also express gratitude to Westphalia Press for their always excellent work, and to my wife, Charlene, who read the manuscript with her keen, proofreader's eye. She caught errors so minor that they escaped even the professional copyreading.

CHAPTER 1

THE ELECTION

The 3rd of November 2020

Here it is, election day. I was barely convinced we'd make it. Bedraggled as we are, though, here we are.

I'm not nervous by nature, but it's hard to wait for the returns to start coming in. Polling, anecdotes, common sense, and in fact, all indications are that this corrupt, divisive, incompetent, and malevolent administration, along with the Republicans, the currently dominant political party that accepted, justified, and enabled it, will be flung from office into oblivion.

And that is essential. A mere win isn't enough—it would be completely inadequate. To hear this president tell it, he expects to be in office for the next term, and beyond. He must go, and there must be absolutely an annihilation of Republicans up and down the ticket. As partisan as that sounds, it's an objective assessment.

So far as I can tell, there is general disgust at the president's rambling and increasingly disjointed comments that seem to get worse every time he makes a public appearance. Even so, he seems pleased with everything he's doing, and no one around him would tell him otherwise, so he rarely hears complaints.

No doubt that's to be expected from one so deluded that he quite seriously looked into the possibility of getting his dour countenance carved onto Mount Rushmore or hoped to receive the Nobel Peace Prize. In that respect, at least, he displayed consistency. His "charity" had served primarily as a personal fund, and its most lurid expenditure was thousands of dollars to commission a portrait of himself. That particular scam lasted nearly three decades, dissolved under a court order, and ultimately cost him $2 million that the court ordered him to pay.

The Republican Party of the United States is the only substantial political party in any of the world's democratic republics that has condemned science, rationality, and fact; that has rejected commitment to the foundations of the state; and has completely discarded any remaining hint of willingness to accept defeat—at the polls, or otherwise. Its sitting president is notorious as a swindler, a failed businessman, falsely presented as a multi-billionaire savant, and a man of the people.

In reality, he's a man only of those people who have gold toilets, and the taste to think of them as elegant.

In the most brazen and un-American action imaginable, their president has deliberately poisoned public discourse, creating hostility toward fair elections and encouraging violence if he fails to get his way. In late July, he shattered all pretense of functioning acceptably by suggesting that the elections should be postponed. He bellowed that reliance on mail-in ballots would make the election the most corrupt and dishonest in history (although he says absentee voting, which he uses and which itself depends on the mail, is fine). This is interesting, coming from a man who has no knowledge of or interest in history, and even less concern for what is and is not acceptable—or truthful.

The unhinged and frantic president produces a constant stream of hysterical tweets. He believes, or pretends to believe, that hordes of unqualified people are rushing to the polls everywhere, eager to cast fraudulent votes. Of course, much of the vote already is in, having been cast early, or put in the mail. No one seems to be paying attention to the orange font of conspiracy theories. That's somewhat surprising, because many on the far right seem to have fervent faith in the abilities of people who hold no office to oppress them. They talk as if they believe that somehow, with a magic akin to that of a malignant Santa Claus, Hillary Clinton and Barack Obama—perhaps accompanied by George Soros—will mysteriously appear in all their houses simultaneously some night to confiscate their firearms.

There have been warnings that this evening will not be a traditional vote-watching night. The pandemic has created such turmoil throughout the country, as it is doing around the world, that it is unlikely, they say, for the returns to be in for us to watch tonight. Instead, we won't know for days.

As things seem to be turning out, though, the election authorities in the thousands of precincts appear to be doing an efficient job, and perhaps we will have a more nearly normal election evening than expected. Voting by mail certainly has helped, and floods of mailed ballots have been coming in for weeks.

Of course, it won't be the end of the world if it were to take days. Elections may be called earlier, but the official results are never ready for several days. In fact, it wouldn't be the first time, even in modern history, if there were a substantial delay. In 2000, the decision that Bush won didn't come until December. The 1876 election decision came even later; Rutherford B. Hayes was declared the winner on the 2nd of March, just before the March 4th inauguration.

It's telling that even Steven Calabresi, the co-founder of the ultra-conservative Federalist Society (more about that later), who has supported conservative policies down the line and who voted for this president, was shocked by the president's assertion that electoral integrity is compromised, and that the elections should be postponed. Breaking at last with the Senate Republicans whom he supported when all but one opted to retain the flawed president after his impeachment, Calabresi said, accurately, that this statement alone is grounds not only for impeachment, but for removal from office.

Shortly after the sitting president's subversive tweet about election postponement, a study reported that a majority of his supporters would refuse to accept the results of the election if he lost, and mail-in ballots had contributed to his defeat. This is disturbing, of course, but it doesn't explain what "refuse to accept" means.

I could say I wouldn't accept the results of an election, regardless of the electoral college, if the victorious candidate failed to win the popular vote. So what? If I do nothing but complain, there is no effect. It would be different—very serious—if I were to try to overthrow the winner.

However it's defined, though, the study's results are cause for concern, yet no one should find them surprising. His supporters have been saying similar things ever since he entered politics. It's hardly a new sentiment among them and does possibly raise the threat of armed rebellion. Statements by Republican candidates darkly warning of the need for "Second-Amendment remedies" if they disagree with electoral results go back at least a decade. Sherron Angle in 2010 used the term when she called for possible resort to violence after voters turned her down as a candidate for the U.S. Senate in Nevada.

In June of 2017, shortly after he took office, the *Washington Post* reported the results of a study by two political scientists revealing that 52% of Republicans would support election postponement, if their president proposed it. The support would rise to 56% if congressional Republicans supported their president's proposal.

This is frightening, and is intended to be, however much such deplorable opinions are in the minority. I try to keep it in perspective, though. Not all of his supporters are so extreme, and all of his supporters together are a minority of the population.

All indications are that there will be an electoral blowout against the Republicans. For civic peace, there has to be. There must be a Biden-Harris victory so enormous that not even hardcore right wingers can plausibly claim foul. Intellectually, I'm confident, but it's always wise to be prepared for the worst.

Anxious though I am, I can't help remembering an experience I had years ago, one that could be an analogy for what the country is going through. It was barely after dawn on a summer day. I foolishly swam too far out into the Gulf from the Florida coast. I was playing in the waves, swimming farther and farther until people on the beach looked like miniatures. I was enjoying myself. I was having fun; too much fun.

Suddenly, with a shock, I recognized I was already in trouble. I felt the first twinges of fatigue. No amount of "distracted swimming" could prevent me from recognizing that going back against the tide would be harder than going out. I needed to do whatever was necessary to get back and needed to start without delay. There were no options. It was to get back however I could or drown. I felt my chances were not good. Adrenaline kicked in. I knew it would be unlikely to be enough to get me back, but, regardless, I simply had to do it.

As a pilot, I would never have flown away from land, with a tailwind, without a huge amount of fuel remaining to return, but I was doing something I was unaccustomed to doing, open-water swimming. I hadn't planned adequately, because I was relying solely on myself, not on an engine I needed to keep going. I was failing to pay attention to my circumstances. I had done the equivalent of using too much gasoline.

I turned back and tried to marshal my energy by taking my time, but that didn't work. I had to swim hard enough to overcome the current to avoid being swept backward, out to sea, and that meant I had to overexert myself. So, on I went, until I reached the point of exhaustion. I could barely move my arms. Once, I almost gave up, accepting the consequences, but I wanted to live. I had things to do, and obligations to fulfill. I was determined, and for whatever reason got a bit of "second wind."

My luck was better than I deserved. I had noticed the swells rising and falling, and finally felt my toes touch sand when the water level fell. With each drop in depth, since my legs were not as exhausted as my arms were, I found I could walk a few steps forward, digging my toes into the sand, then rising up with the water when it rose, and fighting to keep the feet or yards (or inches) I had gained. I kept that up, on and on, until I reached water shallow enough that I could come closer to an actual walk.

I have no idea how long, actually, it took me to make it back to the beach. It must not have been as long as it seemed, but when I got there, I gave in to exhaustion, and collapsed on the welcome ground. I lay there for some minutes, regaining strength until I could stand, and then walk. Of course, I determined that I would never again be so careless. I also vowed I would never let myself be so out of shape. Despite my now advanced age, I never have.

This country has done something far more dangerous. I recovered almost immediately, needing only a brief period of rest. The country will not fully escape the ravages of this savage administration for decades, and many of those who've survived have been damaged beyond the point of recovery, including the administration's supporters. Some of them, in fact, are the most damaged of all—at least the less ignorant and the more politically aware of them. They have sold their souls, and what could cause more damage than that?

America's governing structure is out of shape, as is its electorate. Citizens need to pledge never again to be so foolish, and never again to let their strength—that is, their good judgment, civic awareness, and determination to participate fully—become so feeble that they are in such danger that they seem unable to get out.

Just as I worked to develop strength physically, so must the country turn its attention diligently to building up the civic strength that decades of Republican efforts under the malevolent but effective tutelage of their Newt Gingrichs and Moscow Mitches have deliberately caused to atrophy. They will need to work diligently to develop civic awareness, and to ensure that they are well-prepare to maintain democratic government.

America's voters should have learned from this experience that it is pure self-indulgence to vote because you like or don't like a candidate for president. Like it or not, in every presidential election, only two have any chance at all of being elected: the Republican or Democratic candidate. "I'm tired of voting for the least worst," we heard. Tough. How about contributing to victory by the *worst* worst? That absolutely happened (again) in 2016, thanks to our inexcusable electoral college.

The people should never have to fight so fiercely to get their toes into the electoral sand, simply to survive and get back to the political shore. They should never again let themselves get into such a weakened and vulnerable situation. As it is, already their survival as voters is decidedly at risk; *literally* at risk. "Use it or lose it," applies absolutely to the vote in this bizarre age.

They—we—have made to the point at which we can dig our collective toes into the sand, but we have not yet made it back even to the shallow waters, let alone to the safety of land. We need to see what the voters have said.

Election day is here, and I have to stop this self-flagellation, it gets me nothing anyway. I can accept the good fortune that a long national nightmare, worse than the one that President Gerald Ford rejoiced at being over, also may now be ending ... should now be ending ... and by the grace of God, *will* be ending.

You don't have to be a believer to say, "thank God." We're still wary, though. How could we not be, considering the cascade of disasters that in the short time of one presidential term have changed everything for America, and all for the worst? Most of us expected some of the tragedy, but the system stifled us. Even among those who anticipated the worst, I doubt anyone could have predicted how truly tragic this administration would be.

To look at only one thing, the major health crisis worldwide occasioned by a new scourge, the coronavirus, reveals actions that not even the most unrestrained author of dystopias could ever have envisioned, not even from the most stupid or cruel national leader. Considering that America's record in handling the pandemic is among the world's worst, it's not even an exaggeration to say that its leader actually *has* been the most stupid, *and* cruel, especially since he refuses to take any blame and insists that his record is flawless (when he can remember the word).

Who could have conceived of an American president who would dismantle the existing infrastructure designed to prepare for healthcare emergencies, simply because he was jealous of President Obama, from whom he had inherited it? Could any writer of satire be so unrealistic as to create a leader who would "deal" with a pandemic by: first denying it existed, and then boasting that he had anticipated it long before "the experts"?

Would any reader accept such a character who then claimed that he had handled the pandemic "perfectly," as it raged out of control, and all the while asserting that he was in complete control, but disclaiming any responsibility for the resulting deaths? Could such a writer make his character refuse to act, saying that governors of the states should be the responsible parties, because he wasn't a shipping clerk?

Who could have predicted that any leader, even in a fit of pique, would withdraw the United States *in the midst of the pandemic* from the World Health Organization? His "pandemic program" then would involve continuing the long Republican campaign to rid the country of the Affordable Care Act (the dreaded Obamacare) that was the sole source of health care for millions of Americans—again, *in the midst of a pandemic.*

His government even halted research on preventive treatments and therapy for damaged lungs in the midst of the greatest pulmonary threat in history, as the Biomedical Advanced Research and Development Authority (BARDA) announced quietly on a government website on the 3rd of June. No one could have predicted such things, because hardly any other "leader" in the world, even the most irrational, would have considered them for a second. Writing the record of this insane administration will make historians sound more fanciful than writers of fiction.

Four years ago, millions of us—a substantial majority of the voters—received a collective kick in the gut. The electoral college, with considerable assistance from gerrymandering, partisan Court decisions, actual intimidation, malevolent voter suppression, massive political propaganda, a huge influx of invited Russian meddling, and decades of foul and deceitful lies poured upon Democrats in general and Hillary Clinton in particular ignored the people's clear preference, and elevated to power a bombastic—and obvious—con man.

Those lies were not confined to the 2016 race. The press in 2000 formed a dislike for Al Gore. Accordingly, the herd of commentators uncritically picked up the theme that the vice president was a serial liar (which he was not), who among other things claimed he invented the Internet (which he did not claim).

The con artist won the electoral vote. He had been, and continued to be, obsessed with putting his name on everything, every "tower" he could manage, every food product he could hawk, golf course he could play, airplane he could lease, or even fake enterprise such as a "university" that he could create to soak every possible dollar from the naïve, most especially the gullible poor who could be persuaded to borrow to enrich the pitchman.

In our futile, but at least slightly satisfying bit of civil disobedience, since he has been far worse in reality than the evil Voldemort was in fiction, people some time ago spontaneously began ostentatiously avoiding ever again mentioning or writing his name. This seems to have been a collective and largely unconscious hope that his name—that he plastered everywhere—might somehow be erased from history.

This victorious candidate had failed at business, in his personal life, and everywhere else except that most unreal activity, "reality" television, which rescued him after he ran out of money. He bullied his way through to notoriety, though, with unique brashness, swindling, and outrageous boasts.

This president who-shall-not-be-named functioned much like so many television evangelists who succeed in persuading the poorest people who cannot even pay the rent or afford their prescriptions, first to send everything they could scrape up "for the Lord," so that they, the money magnets on TV, could continue to luxuriate in their corporate jets. Despite "judge not," it's hard not to think that if there is a hell, these monsters all are rushing rapidly toward permanent residence there—even those who have become God's prophets (we have their own statements as assurance that this is true). No wonder they supported their brother in crime when he became President of the United States of America.

In suppressing the votes, Republicans were united in a single principle: don't worry about governing, just hang on to power. Their message was: if you ain't voting Republican, you ain't voting if we can stop it. More often than not, they succeeded, making voting as difficult as they could whenever they could, which is what they did whenever they thought it would be to their advantage.

This isn't just a disgruntled voter grousing. Listen to Republicans, themselves. Usually, they didn't hide it at all. Often, they boasted about it, and even tried to get others to agree that there was nothing wrong with lying, cheating, and stealing. No wonder they had welcomed the orange monster, and handed him their party to use, regardless of the extent of his own bewilderment, as he saw fit.

He was the logical culmination of a once respectable political party that for reasons best known, if at all, only to its leaders, had embarked upon a period of years in which they steadily degenerated. First, they ignored and then forgot about making government work. Then, they ignored and forgot about the public good, leaving themselves free to pursue nothing but power.

If anyone thinks I'm exaggerating, consider this. No one, in fact, should ever forget it. Two Republican officials from North Carolina wrote brazenly in an article in *The Atlantic* (March 25, 2019) that they had crafted the state's congressional districts so that, when the Democrats had received a majority of the state's votes, those Democrats secured only three of North Carolina's thirteen congressional seats while the Republicans obtained ten. The officials explained candidly why they had skewed the system, saying that they restricted the Democrats to three out of thirteen seats, despite a Democratic majority of the votes, because they couldn't figure out how to limit the Democrats to only *two* out of the thirteen seats. They were not joking.

Nor should anyone ignore the politicized conservatives, all members of the Federalist Society, ruling from the U.S. Supreme Court, in *Rucho v. Common Cause,* that such gerrymandering for political gain was fully acceptable. Well, yes, it's acceptable to those who benefit. It should be seen as outrageous to everyone else. Remember, also, that regardless of some occasional decisions that have been decent, the thrust of this Court is to rule consistently in a way that permits Republican states to make it more and more difficult for qualified American citizens to vote.

We expected the worst from the election results in 2016, sure, or at least we thought we did. We had no idea. Whatever we expected, it all became progressively worse than we ever could have dreamed. The widespread feeling of disbelief mixed with nausea has been with us ever since.

Many observers say the election today will be close. It's hard to see why. As I said, I am nervous—or I suppose apprehensive—but to be honest, I am expecting a huge reaction against the thugs who have violated all the principles of politics that have enabled the system to work—not perfectly, certainly, not even adequately for many—but for most of us at least acceptably (that's to our shame, when we think of those whom the system has brutalized).

The reforms that were vital for the rest of us, had seemed at least to be possible until the vandals wrecked everything. So, yes, I think the people's good sense will prevail so much that it can overwhelm the Republican rigging of everything they have touched. Of course, I also expected voter good sense to bring a Hillary victory in 2016 , when there was far less reason for anger. Unfortunately, the Electoral College plus poor turnout overwhelmed the good sense of those who did vote. I am hoping that there has been a "lesson learned," and that it will bring a better result this time.

There has been unprecedented vitriol from the Oval Office, and it has steadily become worse throughout this disastrous administration. Back in May, White House tweets insanely screeched that a TV broadcaster who had criticized the administration was a murderer, referring to a natural death twenty years before, at a time when the broadcaster was 900 miles away. Even supporters were uncomfortable with that, and it got worse when the unhinged president raged two weeks ago that Joe Biden had shot Rush Limbaugh.

Limbaugh had just died, and he was in Florida—Biden was not—and it was clear that Limbaugh was not the victim of violence but had succumbed to his well-publicized lung cancer. Not even his Presidential Medal of Freedom, cynically awarded in a unique travesty, could save him—nor could he take it with him.

The emperor's lack of clothes should have been apparent to any sentient being, but nevertheless, his base persisted. Happily, though, at least a few of them have peeled away, shrinking their bulk. The outrageous Franklin Graham and Jerry Falwell, Jr., have lost much of their following; enough so that their empires are crumbling. Falwell was first to go after he had posted photos of himself, on a yacht, no less, that made the ancient photo of Gary Hart on the boat Monkey Business seem quaintly innocent by contrast, although it killed Hart's 1988 presidential bid.

This president boasts of any action being an accomplishment that was a first, the biggest ever, or the most of something (bigly?) that no other president could accomplish. Well, he very nearly accomplished a genuine first. Because of his erratic and inexcusable behavior, he came close to being the only president who ever had been impeached twice—and in only one term. It was so close to the election, though, that Speaker Pelosi persuaded House Democrats not to go that route, but simply to wait for the election, hoping for a thorough cleansing.

How can his support exist at all, when his incompetence created massive chaos, paving the way for the Covid-19 pandemic? Hundreds of thousands of Americans have died during these years from administration policy, policy that was stupid at best and deliberate at worst. No other country in the world has had as many deaths from Covid-19 as has the United States.

The tweeting president had denied it would happen, ignoring all warnings and lying constantly until illness and death overwhelmed the health system. With its leadership in over its collective head, the country found itself in a conglomeration of its most tumultuous experiences: a great depression, a threat to its health, a powerful civil rights movement, the Me Too movement, and the worst income disparity in modern history. This was thanks to the one who campaigned as the "only one who could fix things." Some fixing. It was to be expected, of course, from one who knew absolutely nothing about what he was doing or was supposed to be doing.

Early on the president had said everything was in order to handle anything, so we should cut, cut, cut the healthcare budget. Then, coronavirus hit. He then whined when he found himself not knowing what to do, that he had been left with an empty cupboard. Never has he explained, of course, why he eliminated, rather than added to, the arsenal that should have been well-stocked to combat any pandemic.

Well, enough musing. The returns are beginning to come in.

As I admitted, I'm nervous. I hesitate to be optimistic. I don't want to be crushed, but things do appear to be going well with the electorate. Turnout seems to be extraordinary. Even, where there are plentiful polling stations—all in states Democrats control, of course—the lines have been incredible despite the pandemic. In Republican states, where stringent efforts have done everything that evil genius can conjure up to restrict voting, and where places to vote are rare, at least in areas that the Republicans think might vote Democratic, the crowds waiting to vote are unprecedented. In fact, in some such states the crowds of citizens demanding to vote are waiting with determined patience, promising to set records for turnout. Voters in those areas are giving every indication that they will stay and vote, if they have to wait all week, while Republicans give every indication of trying to assure that they will, indeed, have to wait that long.

Early voting, absentee voting, vote by mail, all seem to be joining with voting in person to ensure that the numbers of voters will break the records. As polls in eastern states began to close, early in the evening, it seemed as though a blue wave were coming. Astonishingly, all those on the coast, from the extremes of north (Maine) to those on the south (Florida) went for Biden-Harris.

Among them, voters in states that had Republican legislatures or Republican governors up for election, replaced them with Democrats. Those that had Republican senators up for re-election: Maine (the faux moderate Susan Collins), North Carolina (Thom Tillis), South Carolina (the ineffable, pearl-clutching, presidential henchman, Lindsey Graham), and Georgia (David Perdue, and the stock-selling Kelly Loeffler; the state had two seats up because of a special election for Leoffler's seat) rejected the Republicans, and voted in Democrats. That electoral vote trove, Florida, with no governor or senator up for re-election, despite outrageous gerrymandering, went Democratic by voting for Biden, and also for Democratic majorities in both houses of the legislature.

Proceeding westward, Alabama's Democratic senator Doug Jones was thought to be the most endangered Democrat, but won by a decent majority, while Alabama, fueled by enthusiastic Black women, exhibited that it was moving in the direction of common sense, and voted for Biden-Harris. Astonishingly, all states east of the Mississippi River, voted for Biden-Harris and, where there was a contest voted for Democratic senators as well. Even Mississippi itself, the state, voted for Democrats (there was a slight harbinger of this in July, at least in retrospect, when Mississippi's legislature and governor agreed to remove the racist Confederate battle flag emblem from the state's constitution). Causing perhaps the greatest joy about the congressional vote among Democrats was the defeat in Kentucky of the infamous "Moscow Mitch" McConnell, the Republican leader of the U. S. Senate. Tennessee, following the delightful pattern, filled its open Senate seat with a Democrat.

The three states with tiny margins for the Republican presidential candidate in 2016, Pennsylvania, Michigan, and Wisconsin went for Biden-Harris with comfortable majorities, regaining their previous status as the "blue wall." They also demonstrated their growing enlightenment by going for Democratic majorities in their legislatures. That took a huge wave, in view of the gerrymanders that Democrats had to overcome. The generally Republican state of Ohio (without which no Republican had ever been elected president), joined them.

The 4th of December 2020

By midnight, it had become clear that "blue wave" was an understatement. The year 2020 has been the year of presidential outrages, the tragic coronavirus pandemic, economic disasters, and increasing violence including police murders of unarmed black people, and the imposition of militarized forces on cities controlled by Democrats. It's almost as though those in power were abusing it so thoroughly as to sneer aloud that you can't stop us!

But just as if the year itself were chagrined and as if it were apologizing as it was fading into history, it attempted to give us some compensation. It would be the year of the enormous blue tsunami. States in the middle of the country were all going for Biden-Harris. As the clock advanced, so, too, did the Biden-Harris victories, the Democratic victories in legislatures, governorships, and in the U.S. Senate.

The existing administration was simply too inept, too dangerous, too outrageous, and frankly too embarrassing for even the most hardcore red states to stomach. State after state was called for Biden-Harris. In red states, the minority Democrats, thoughtful independents, and disgruntled Republicans joined to return reason, stability, and competence to government. The blue inundation swept toward the Pacific, and jumped to include Hawaii (of course), but even Alaska as well.

As the sun came up Wednesday morning, I was too elated even to feel sleepy (although when I went to bed shortly thereafter, I crashed). Most states that had legislative chambers that were controlled by Republicans voted Democrats in as the majority. Only a few states were left with Republican legislatures; Republican governors were an endangered species.

Twenty-three of the sitting U.S. senators running were Republicans. Most of them were running for seats thought to be safe. With one exception, all lost to Democrats. Even Kansas, which had an open Senate seat, voted in a Democrat. It was the first time Kansas voted for a Democratic senator since 1932.

The exception to the Democratic wave of new senators was Senator Ben Sasse, Republican of Nebraska, who survived the disaster that befell other Republicans. He was lucky in his opponent, who remained on the ballot despite having been asked to withdraw by Nebraska's Democratic Party. The Democratic opponent was the owner of a small business. He had made it clear even if anyone seriously thought he was a rocket scientist, that (sadly for the Democrats) he was not the ideal candidate. He had sent sexually explicit messages ("she needs to get laid," or something to that effect) to his staffers. This would hardly have been wise conduct any time (or even marginally acceptable, although the sitting president had done worse, and still had won office), but it clearly was idiotic—if not a political death wish—in the midst of a campaign for public office.

Something else that was truly historical had taken place, thanks to the Republican recklessness and arrogance that had given succor to the worst administration in history. Only two presidents had carried all the states: George Washington and James Monroe. Washington had garnered every possible electoral vote; Monroe in 1820, all but one, which went to John Quincy Adams, who had not even been a candidate.

The myth arose that the one electoral vote that didn't go to Monroe went to Adams because the elector, William Plumer of New Hampshire, wanted to maintain Washington as the only president to have received 100% of the possible electoral votes. Plumer's son, however, said it wasn't true. Plumer just didn't like Monroe.

Regardless, Biden-Harris carried all fifty states. People liked Joe Biden and were excited by Kamala Harris. Probably more important, though, they had come to loathe, despise, fear, and disdain the sitting president. Democrats already controlled the U. S. House, and they picked up nearly 100 additional seats there, ousting even the wingnut fringes, such as presidential hench-men Jim Jordan of Ohio and Devin Nunes of California.

Happily, it was no longer necessary to worry about the racist loudmouth from Iowa, Steve King, because he, mercifully, after a lengthy and disreputable 18 years in the House, had already lost his primary. Even House Republicans had shunned him. As a reminder, he was the one who had seemed sincerely befud-dled about why white supremacy had (in his mind "suddenly") become unacceptable.

The 22-seat pickup in the Senate meant that in Congress, Dem-ocrats in the next session would control more than two-thirds of each House, enough to *propose* constitutional amendments. Equally important, the elections brought Democrats to pow-er in more than three-fourths of the states, which meant that they controlled enough states to *ratify* proposed constitutional amendments. They also would be in position to draw fair dis-trict boundaries and rid the country of the shame of grossly political gerrymanders that Republicans had left as their me-morials.

All that presupposed, of course, that the Democrats would act together. There were hopeful signs that they would, although party history had been notoriously fractious, typified by the quip long ago from the now late humorist, Will Rogers, that he was not a member of any organized political party—he was a Democrat. (Although this likely is totally irrelevant, it's at least interesting that this Oklahoma cowboy had been named for the Quaker founder of Pennsylvania, William Penn.) Happily, Nancy Pelosi, arguably the most able speaker of the House in history, would be able to coordinate House Democrats skillfully.

Democrats and all who savor good government—even those who were not especially concerned about politics, but who just miss a feeling that government just might work sometimes for them, and that could apply to a huge mass of citizens of good will—could imagine a resounding cheer, from the entire country as the land considered Joe Biden and Kamala Harris, receiving the unanimous votes of the electors. The imaginary cheer would modulate into an imaginary roar of approval, when the mass of people contemplated that the buffoonish president who bragged constantly that everything he did was the best ever, unquestionably turned a showing that was the *worst* ever.

In a close election, the Republicans would try anything—and might actually succeed—in questioning the outcome or finding some way to shift the results so that they would win. That surely could only happen, though, in a close election, such as that in Florida in 2000, or in the three wayward states of Wisconsin, Michigan, and Pennsylvania in 2016, when they garnered tiny margins that corrupted the electoral college outcome to ignore the popular will. We Democrats assured ourselves that would be impossible in such an overwhelming election, with both the popular vote and the all-important electoral vote reflecting the completely clear outcome. We began to rest comfortably. We were secure.

To be fair, it was not "the people" who had fallen for the con by the surprise Republican nominee in 2016. The people at that time voted, by a substantial majority, for Hillary Clinton. Like her or not, she would have been enormously capable, and without doubt she was the most well-prepared candidate for a first presidential term in history. It was the electoral college that shunted aside the people's will and installed literally the least well-prepared candidate in history—the least well-prepared not only in terms of background and preparation, but also in character, intelligence, judgment, empathy, and integrity.

We the people, collectively, now have assured that he soon will be gone, and have redressed the misbehavior of the electoral college. "It Couldn't Happen Here,"? It didn't. Not three-quarters of a century ago when Sinclair Lewis asked ironically in the title of his novel, warning that it might; nor now, except for one brief (but still too long) presidential term when the country that had gone a step farther and its antiquated and dangerous system, over the peoples' objections, had installed a would-be fascist in the White House. That fascist will be gone when his term ends on the 20th of January. If we can make it this far through such a deplorable administration, surely we can last through the next few weeks until a rational administration headed by Biden and Harris, takes office. We're resilient!

This was the blue tsunami we had hoped to see. When I went to sleep that night, I must have been smiling.

CHAPTER 2

THE FLAWED CONSTITUTION

The 14th of December, 2020

My euphoria didn't last long. The alarm clock blared, ruining my sleep. For several reasons, I awoke feeling strange, partly because I never use an alarm. I'm sure I hadn't set it. Ah well, I must have hit the button accidentally. I almost always awake early, so it hardly matters.

Getting back to the election, I felt unsettled. I awoke wondering if I had been right to be wary. Checking my sources, I found that however damaging the blow they received, Republicans immediately after the election began to regroup, emboldened by a few contributions from diehard billionaires (justly fearing tax increases). They fought as viciously to hang on to power as they could figure out how. In the days to come, I had followed their every step. Nothing they did came as a surprise. They were inventive, I had to admit, though all it took was a knowledge of the Constitution and a complete lack of restraint, civil commitment, or conscience. Following their president and the soon-to-be ousted Senate leader, Moscow Mitch McTraitor—along with Newt Gingrich and other assorted bottom feeders—they began to wage total war. Heedless of what it might do to their country, they plotted to go nuclear, in a political sense.

Shortly after the historic victory of the Democrats, electing their candidates to nearly all positions in national, state, and local governments, Republicans began to hold meetings. These were secret at first, but word leaked out almost immediately, so soon they began to flaunt them, and boast that they could overcome anything.

His opponents had been fearful that the president would refuse to accept the results of any election that rejected him, and
determine to stay in office. Those fears had subsided, because
of the enormous defeat that he had suffered. No president
in history had been so soundly, and thoroughly, repudiated.
The 2020 defeat of the most ill-suited president ever to occu-
py the White House had made poor William Taft's 1912 loss
(Taft carried only Vermont and Utah) seem by contrast to
have been almost a triumph (considering that Taft faced two
giants, Theodore Roosevelt and the odious—from my point
of view—segregationist Woodrow Wilson). The popular vote
was roughly 61% for Biden-Harris, about equaling that record
set by Lyndon B. Johnson-Hubert Humphrey in 1964 (in presidential races, only LBJ, Richard Nixon in 1972, Franklin D.
Roosevelt in 1936, and Warren Harding [!] in 1920 had ever
touched 60%; not even the most overrated president in history, at least among Republicans, the sainted Ronald Reagan had
achieved that triumph).

As for the important count, the electoral vote, Biden-Harris had
won all 538; they had needed only 270. In any case, a president
does not have to accept defeat to be defeated. The incumbent at
the end of his term could be escorted from office unceremoni-
ously, if he were to attempt to ignore the outcome. The winner
becomes president at noon on the 20th of January, regardless of
what the former president does, or does not do, or accept.

As it turned out, however, verifying the worst fears of those who
were nervous, the president needed to pull no shenanigans. The
Constitution clearly provided the Republicans, who long ago
had discarded any thought of playing by the accepted rules of
the game, the weapon to hang on to power. Without question,
I hate to say it, but I have to admit that the Republicans were
correct legally, if not ethically or morally. Constitutional provisions did empower them. The Constitution specified that

24

the incumbent president would retain the office until noon on the 20ᵗʰ of January following the election, that is, in 2021. The old Congress continued to be in place until noon on the 3ʳᵈ of January. The Democrats would not become the majority in the Senate until Noon on the 3ʳᵈ of January, and the winner of the election would not become president until noon of the 20ᵗʰ of that month.

Things were similar around the country. Most new state legislatures did not come into office until the new year, which meant that Republicans would continue to control the legislatures of all those states that had voted for the Republican in 2016. Some of those states already had Democratic governors, but their legislatures would remain under the control of Republicans, through the year 2020, despite having been defeated.

They were lame ducks, but they still had full power. As it turned out, they remained empowered; quite dangerously so. The most damaging provision was the infernal electoral college. True, Biden had won all the soon-to-be-cast electoral votes. That, anticipation, though, is based on the modern practice of voters choosing presidential electors, as every one of the states had mandated. Nevertheless, the Supreme Court in its infamous *Bush* v *Gore* decision had said in 2000, with no hint of ambiguity, that the Constitution grants state legislatures the full power to choose electors. The people themselves have no such constitutional right, and as the Court said, the Founders didn't give them one.

Not only did the Court say that, "The individual has no federal constitutional right to vote for electors for the president of the United States unless and until the state legislature chooses a statewide election as the means to implement its power to appoint members of the electoral college," but it made the point that the legislature can at any time go back on any promise it makes about choosing electors. "The state legislature's power to select the manner for appointing electors is plenary; it may, if it so chooses, select the electors itself." It can do so, even if it had permitted the voters to choose, but decided it doesn't like what the voters did.

Most people were justifiably astonished to discover that even after an election, the legislature "can take back the power to appoint electors." It can overturn an election even if the state's own constitution empowers its voters to make the decision. I knew all this in 2000 after the Republicans made sure that Florida's electoral votes would be for Bush, even if a recount were to show that Gore won the state. The legislature at the time actually was planning to submit electoral votes for Bush-Cheney no matter what, even if it were to become clear that Gore had won throughout Florida. The legislature didn't have to be so in-your-face, though, because a Republican Supreme Court stepped in and did it for them. Essentially, what the Court said was, Bush is going to win, so quit trying.

Whatever the legislature wants regarding the electors, the legislature gets. Popular votes don't matter. So instead of being surprised, I actually had expected the defeated Republicans at least to attempt to pull the same stunt. And indeed they did. And indeed they succeeded.

Today, the 14th of December, 2020, the electoral votes went to Congress to be counted. All the states that had voted Republican in 2014 against Hillary Clinton, cast their votes in 2020 for the discredited Republicans who had lost instead of for Biden who had been thoroughly victorious. Thus, an electoral vote majority favoring the incumbent went forth to Washington, just as it had done four years previously.

The counting will take place during the first week of January, at a joint meeting of the two Houses of Congress, the President of the Senate, that is the Vice President, presiding. Since it occurs in the first week of January, the incumbent vice president (his term, remember, lasts until noon on the 20th) will be the presiding official. Any hopes that Democrats retain that something might happen to the count and place the people's choice in power were grasping at straws. The new Democratically-controlled Congress could, of course, reject the vice president's count and reject the entire process, but it would cause a severe constitutional crisis, and in our system, only Republicans, not Democrats, conduct themselves in that manner.

The 4th of January 2021

The entire country is watching the televised proceedings of the joint session of Congress. The newly-elected members have taken their seats (that would have happened yesterday, the 3rd, but that was Sunday). Although he lost in every state, the sitting vice president, Pence, still, for the moment, is in office, and is presiding. The question is whether the Democrats, who control both the House and the Senate overwhelmingly, will find some way to reject enough of the stolen Republican electoral votes to install Joe Biden as president.

Being Democrats, and reluctant to follow Republican precedent, it is becoming clear that the electoral vote count will go against Biden. Just as I am writing, it has done so. Democrats, historically, have rolled over and accepted the outcome, however outrageous, of Republican malfeasance. It appears as if they have done so once more; perhaps not, however. Now, almost immediately after the vote, the newly-elected House is reconvening as a separate body. The members are moving without delay, to vote on an impeachment resolution. As expected, it just passed overwhelmingly. The president and vice president have just been impeached. That becomes the second time that this president has been impeached. He can legitimately claim a first here. The articles of impeachment are going immediately to the Senate.

The previous Senate had had its chance in early 2020 to clear up the mess and rid the country of a monstrously ill-suited president, but it failed in its duty. In early February, it voted to acquit without even hearing a witness. All Democrats voted to convict, but all Republicans, except Utah Senator Mitt Romney, voted to acquit, and conviction would have required two-thirds of the votes. This time, though, more than two-thirds of the senators were Democrats. The new Congress had taken office on the 4th.

The 21st of January 2021

The president's inauguration was set for noon (it would have happened yesterday, but that was Sunday). He had hoped for an enormous crowd, and indeed it was huge.

It wasn't what he wanted, though. By far, most of those there were protestors.

Most of them probably were aware that they were to witness history in the making. It's doubtful, though, that anyone that day had any real sense of just how historical—and in fact how politically bizarre—the day would become.

The new Senate had convened early that morning as a court, to try the impeachments. After being rushed to the proceedings, the chief justice was presiding, since the president was on trial, and the vice president's trial was simultaneous. Otherwise, if it had been held separately, the vice president, Pence, would have presided over his own trial. That fact should demonstrate even to constitutional fundamentalists that the Founders were not perfect. The senators waited. They took no vote until noon, but they resisted any move by the chief justice to create a formal delay.

Precisely at noon, the moment the new terms began, the Senate voted. They had no trouble getting to the vote that the Constitution requires: two-thirds of those present, and they all were there. The vote to convict was overwhelming. At completion of the vote, the offices of president and vice president became vacant. Speaker of the House Nancy Pelosi, at that same time, became acting president.

Her first act took place while she still was in the Capitol Building. That was to submit the name of Joseph Biden to the House and Senate for confirmation as Vice President of the United States. Both Houses speedily confirmed him on a voice vote, and he was sworn in immediately. Former Vice President Biden had again become Vice President.

As soon as President Pelosi had her vice president duly confirmed, she resigned as president. Vice President Biden at that instant became what the voters had intended: he became President of the United States, Joseph Biden.

Fox News, right-wing radio, and Franklin Graham seethed in anger (Jerry Falwell, Jr., probably did too, but after his disgrace he no longer was in the picture). That's not fair, they screamed, with the evangelicals throwing in that Democrats obviously were going against God's will as expressed by his agency on earth, the sacred Electoral College.

Meanwhile, after her resignation as president, Nancy Pelosi was immediately welcomed back to the House as Speaker. A few isolated voices shouted in anger. All the shouts came from the handful of Republicans still in the House. They protested that Pelosi could not be speaker. She could not even be seated, because she was no longer a member of the House. They said that when she became president, even though her presidency had lasted less than a day, she had immediately surrendered her seat as a representative from California when she accepted it.

She conceded the point; she said she had to agree that she had given up her seat when she accepted the presidency. The House Democrats agreed, as well. She was no longer a representative, and they would not act unfairly or improperly, and try to claim that she was.

What they had done was to anticipate that objection.

It was correct that Pelosi no longer was a representative, but that was irrelevant. Despite their stridency and their legal arguments, Pelosi had no trouble regaining her position as speaker. The Democrats knew they were on solid ground, not merely because they now had overwhelming control, but they knew that the Constitution was clear on the matter. They had sought legal opinion to verify that this was the case. All authorities consulted agreed.

Although every speaker has been a member of the House of Representatives, the Constitution does not require it. The House chooses its speaker, says the Constitution, but nothing in that Constitution limits the House's selection to an elected representative, nor does the Constitution prescribe any qualifications. All speakers have in fact been representatives, but representatives may choose whomever they wish, regardless. They did so, and Nancy Pelosi stepped again into the speakership.

She had made history not only as the first speaker to have served as president, but she also had become the first speaker not to be a member of the House. She made history in another way as well: her presidential term of two hours, 51 minutes, was the shortest in history, making William Henry Harrison's one month as president before dying in office appear lengthy by contrast.

California's Governor Newsome that day called for a new election to fill the vacant seat to take place as soon as it could be arranged. Pelosi filed as a candidate, and all observers were certain that she would be re-elected, and restored to her seat. As it turned out, no one even filed against her, and thus she was restored to the House by a unanimous vote of the electorate of her San Francisco district. Speaker Pelosi again became once again a duly elected member of Congress.

As soon as he took office, President Biden nominated his running mate, Senator Kamala Harris, to be vice president, and submitted her nomination to Congress. Both Houses confirmed her speedily. Vice President Harris thus became the first female, African-American, and Asian-American vice president.

Thus, the people's will, under the terms of the Constitution and despite the document's flaws, was honored. The candidates they overwhelmingly had favored had become president and vice president of the United States. This was just as the voters intended, in contrast to the outcome of the nightmare election of 2016. The American people had become furious at the electoral college, its ability to overturn the stated will of the people, and Republican willingness to exploit its flaws to maintain themselves in power after they had been voted out. Two of the previous five elections were two too many.

The recent abomination—the near success of the Republican theft—was the breaking point. The people had been patient far too long. That applies especially to America's Black and Brown citizens who had borne the greatest injustice from the warped election college selections, just as they had borne the burden of police brutality. The electoral college had to go, and Democratic power now was sufficient to improve the Constitution.

The people finally had been victorious, but it had required more than a landslide vote to accomplish. It was the first time that their vote had been able to overturn the distorted conclusion of the electoral college. Happily, it had been done in complete accord with the Constitution. It was truly historical, possibly the most politically historical day in America's existence. It likely had been the oddest day as well. It was hard to believe. It was even harder to believe, because I had a sudden thought.

It jarred me into a few seconds of confusion.

The Supreme Court had reached a decision in *Chiafalo* v. *Washington* on the 6th of July, that cited "a longstanding tradition in which electors are not free agents; they are to vote for the candidate whom the State's voters have chosen."

That was before the election. How had all this happened?

Memory of the Court's decision brought me back to reality. I was in bed.

I suddenly was awake. My bedside clock said it was 5:45 am.

The alarm didn't sound. As I had thought, I never set it, and didn't this time. I recognized that I had become so preoccupied for so long with the electoral outcome that I had just had the most elaborate—and elaborately fevered—dream of my life. This happened no doubt because I had feared Republican malfeasance, and had forgotten in the dream that the Court, shortly before, had headed off that possibility.

It took me a brief while before I could clear my mind of confusion.

I wouldn't even mention this strange mental exercise except to call attention to the need to be well-informed, and to keep a close watch on all things political. The dream pointed out how important it is to be vigilant. Its scenario might have been implausible, but so had the election outcomes in 2000 and especially 2016 been. When my full consciousness returned, I recognized that it still was only the 14th of December, the day the electors were to meet in their respective state capitals and cast their votes. By the time they had done so, Joe Biden had become the president-elect; Kamala Harris, the vice president elect.

My alarmist fears, in the immortal words of Ron Zeigler, when he was Nixon's press secretary, had "been inoperable."

CHAPTER 3

HOW DEMOCRATS LEARNED HOW TO FUNCTION APPROPRIATELY FOR THE TWENTY-FIRST CENTURY

I have to continue this narrative, so after a quick breakfast—coffee is the most important part—I made myself begin writing. At first my kitten wanted to help, by walking across the keys. Actually, she now is more of an old lady, but she still seems kittenish to me. I diverted her with a spoonful of strained beef baby food. Each of us has our morning rituals. I was at fault for having delayed hers. Back to work!

Undoubtedly, defeating the oaf who had been president for four years, inflicting his malevolent incompetence on the entire country, not to mention the rest of the world, had been the first order of business. After that, though, people kept asking me what to expect.

"Sure, things were better under Democrats," they often said to me, "and nothing could be so bad as the four years we have just gone through. I'll grant you that. Hey, though, we've had Democratic presidents before, and things still weren't perfect to put it mildly."

They were right, but that was irrelevant. Ever since it began to move in the direction of civil rights, the Democratic Party had been far better across the board than their rival Republicans. To say that they needed improvement was correct, but a flawed friend is far better than an overtly evil enemy. The Democrats had much to learn, and gave every indication that they were doing so, they were going in the direction they needed to go.

As a student and professor of politics for many years, I have kept close watch on the parties and their programs, their strengths and weaknesses. I am under no illusions. I have learned many things in my lengthy career, nearly all of which served to correct the extreme conservative assumptions that came naturally to me as a child because of my heritage and surroundings. I'll discuss a few of the important things I discovered that should help to make the reasons for my thought clear. Fundamentally, much of the correction flows simply from common sense.

Big money tainted Democrats too, and at least the more conservative among them for quite some time tended along with Republicans to be carried away by cries of "law and order," instead of "social justice." For too many post-New Deal Democrats, these unjustified but popular themes tainted their overall views of society and politics. Sometimes they recognized their racism, but more often they harbored unconscious rationalizations that kept their racism covert and hidden even from themselves. They undergirded statements such as, "I'm not racist, but ..." With all their shortcomings, though, they tended to retain more of a conscience than the Republicans who had long since shorn themselves of that inconvenient emotion. Well, perhaps not all emotion. Generally, Republicans skillfully retained hate, especially hatred of Democrats, or perhaps even worse RINOs (Republicans in name only).

The Republican Party, founded to block the expansion of human chattel slavery, began on the side of the angels, but later came to incorporate the worst of the old Democratic Party. For a time, before the New Deal, Republicans remained the better party on civil rights—not that either party was great. Until the New Deal, the worst racism tended to remain within the Democrats, but that began to change among them with the New Deal. After World War II, the loudest political voices for civil rights consistently came from Democrats, although with great resistance from southerners. The new approach among Democrats outside the south was reflected in President Harry Truman's great move desegregating the military by executive order (the racist southern Democrats controlling Congress would never have accepted it). Additionally, there was a great civil rights speech that the Minneapolis Mayor, Hubert Humphrey gave to the 1948 Democratic National Convention.

Republicans worsened through time, stung especially in the 1960s by civil rights. They came close to becoming themselves what their party, and their first president, the admirable Abraham Lincoln, came into politics to oppose.

The "southern strategy" under Nixon and Reagan—with Roy Cohn hovering malignantly hidden by shadows in the background—had sent Republicans on the road to perdition, and prepared the way for Newt Gingrich—filling in for the devil incarnate—who convinced them that politics should be total warfare with all notion of war crimes thrown out the window. "Give no quarter," at least implicitly, became the Republican slogan. That, of course, is a war crime.

Democrats had become the party of civil rights and anti-poverty, proclaimed eloquently by Lyndon Johnson. They were too slow, though, to recognize systemic racism, general injustices toward racial minorities, the poor, and also toward women. There were admirable exceptions, of course, but when Democrats in general began to recognize their failures, they characteristically were far too timid to take effective action, and for far too long. After LBJ, and especially after they had found Reagan so frightening, Democrats had far less fire in their collective bellies in pursuing programs to benefit the people than Republicans had in suppressing anything designed to help.

Democrats, sadly, became almost as likely as Republicans to be misguided by conventional wisdom. They became far more likely than Republicans to be overly cautious, more reluctant to be perceived as out of the mainstream, and more sensitive to criticism. This caution muted their progressivism. Republican vigor was for pernicious policies. Timid progressives, though, still are far better than those who pursue evil policies vigorously.

Fortunately, as they passed beyond this century's first decade, the Democratic Party began to change. Elements in the Party began to recognize that much of what motivated the conventional wisdom, however incessant, was nothing more than lavishly funded, right-wing propaganda designed to protect the wealthy. For example, even among Democrats during the 2020 campaign, it was common among some who should have known better, to refer to "radicals, such as those favoring Medicare for all, or the Green New Deal." However extreme those may appear to some, it's really laughable. Those policies hardly are radical. Almost everyone recognizes that Medicare works far better than private insurance, and its beneficiaries love it. How many can say that about their HMOs? Therefore, if it is good for the elderly, why not it, or something similar or preferably better, for others?

It would be far better than American healthcare delivery prior to the Affordable Care Act, but that doesn't mean it would be the best way to go. Stronger arguments can support a completely nationalized version of Medicaid for all, although as Senator Sanders and others had suggested, Medicare with greatly expanded benefits, shorn of its privatized features and of co-pays and limitations, could be excellent as well. Medicaid would have fewer ingrained features to eliminate.

As for the Green New Deal, initially there obviously are two considerations: first, social programs such as those in the New Deal with additions from FDR's Economic Bill of Rights are a bare minimum to deal with the reality, and ultimate aftermath, of the coronavirus, as well as systematic injustice, economic and otherwise. Even before the pandemic, the need was far greater than conservatives or even some progressives recognized. Second, it also is absolutely essential—crucial—to become effectively active in combatting climate change. The planet's future well-being requires it, so the Green New Deal, far from being radical, is common sense. This time, with a new and dedicated administration, things really were going to be different. It came as a shock to many citizens when they realized the elaborate framework crafted to protect the people from the privileged and incorporated in the rhetoric of the Revolution had morphed through the years into a framework that worked to protect the privileged from the people. It then became clear that much public discourse had been ideology presented as analysis. Social Security, for example, was not "going broke." It never had been, and never could. Small government, despite its hallowed spot in the country's mythology, was not, in fact, the best at governing. In reality, it did not govern well at all, never had, never would, and becomes ever more inadequate as technology, and corporate industrialization, intensify.

The debt ceiling is another example that should have been obvious as serving no purpose except to make mischief possible. Putting a ceiling on debt might appear to hold down spending, but it doesn't. It only places obstacles in the way of paying bills for money already spent. I'll get around to this later, but there should be no debt ceiling, which is fraudulent. Congress does not need to be borrowing at all. At the national level, the government does not need to borrow to pay its bills, nor does paying its bills even require it to tax. Taxes are important, but taxation is not necessary to pay the national government's bills.

Whatever rationale may have existed in 1917 when the idea of a debt ceiling was legislated into law has long since vanished. No longer are there limitations on Congress, such as a gold standard, that prevent it from creating dollars as it wishes, but regardless of that, the way to restrict spending certainly is not to refuse to pay the bills that come due, which is precisely what the debt ceiling purports to do.

Congress appropriates money to pay its bills. When those bills come due, it generally issues bonds—that is, it borrows—to get the money to pay its obligations. If that borrowing needs to exceed the arbitrary limit on debt, Congress raises the debt ceiling to accommodate the borrowing. Congress is obligated to pay the bills, regardless of any limitation. Except for the truly unhinged, even budget hawks who detest government spending do not argue that the US should default, so the debt ceiling is a complete sham. All it accomplishes at best is to permit members of Congress to present themselves as "fiscally responsible." At worst, it can become a hostage for an irresponsible senator willing to oppose raising it until something desired is first approved. That is, it enables such a senator to threaten government default in order to bully others to submit.

I grew up as a conservative, an arch conservative actually, in an extremely conservative family, in the most conservative section, of an irrationally ultra-conservative state. I was a young adult before the application of common sense led me first to question, and then quickly to depart from, my conservative beliefs. It helped, too, when I became better informed by deep study of politics, history, literature, and other subjects—although as we all know, better information doesn't guarantee better judgment. Confirmation bias reigns!

Beginning many years ago, I recognized that common sense alone questioned the dogma of American small-government conservatives. Seeing through their cant required no specialized knowledge, or keen analytical skills. The truth is accessible to anyone willing to question, and not live in fear of being thought "out of the mainstream." To anyone, that is, who becomes well-informed, is thoughtful, and who does not ignore common sense.

Throughout a long career of writing, teaching, and administering I ultimately oriented my writing to reflect what should be obvious to anyone well-versed in American history and politics. In 2017, I built a book, *Unworkable Conservatism*, around a key observation: what passes for conservatism in the United States is different from classic conservatism elsewhere, to a large extent reflecting a form of right-wing liberalism, libertarianism, and anti-government ideology. That is well-known; nothing new here. The unfortunate new aspect is that it is clear that the ideas that American "conservatives" profess don't work. First, they are almost impossible to implement. Consider two prime examples: first, the presidency of Ronald Reagan, and second, the fate of the Affordable Care Act (to Republicans, the infamous "Obamacare").

Reagan was the darling of the hard right. Although it is largely forgotten, until he secured the Republican nomination for president in 1980, Reagan had been considered a right-wing extremist with overly simplistic and unrealistic views upon which he would be unlikely to compromise. Even his supporters were likely to agree that he, like Goldwater who had gone down to a crushing defeat, was a right-wing extremist—because that was precisely what they wanted. Those supporters—in the sexist, ageist, classist, and misogynist slang of the day that definitely misread the appeal of the hard right—were dismissed as largely "little old ladies in tennis shoes." That changed when a major party nominated him, and thus shifted the political ideology of American politics decidedly to the right, making Reagan a respected American political leader.

Regardless, Reagan's hard-core supporters were never satisfied.

41

They always wanted more. Policies they regarded as unsatisfactory were lacking only because they were insufficiently conservative. Unable to bring themselves to criticize the heralded St. Ronnie, they could only blame others. I am old enough to remember their plaintive cries, cries that his aides should "let Reagan be Reagan!"

With regard to the Affordable Care Act, every Republican running for national office in 2016 called for its immediate repeal. The victorious GOP held the presidency and vice presidency, control of the Court, and for two years held control of Congress, both the House and the Senate. Nevertheless, throughout that disastrous reign of ideologues, despite their control of all levers of government, the far-right could not get it done. Every one of their numerous efforts to repeal "Obamacare," failed. Reagan had hated Social Security, and had long advocated its elimination before he ran for the presidency. Early in his first term, he launched an attack on the system. The resulting outcry was so great that he had to promise never again to attack Social Security. The Affordable Care Act, although weakened by persistent attacks, survives.

These examples should call into question any confidence in conservatism, because measures the "conservatives" advocate generally cannot even be enacted, and if they are, they tend to be highly unpopular.

The Democratic Party, whether overtly or implicitly, recognized the truth that what passes for conservatism in America, is, in fact, unworkable. My book was not highly influential, certainly, but it contributed to the mix that led to the Party's enlightenment. You can't defeat Republicans from the right, and if you could, there would be no point. You would have become the thing that you were opposing, and the resulting policies would be detrimental to the people as a whole. Conservatism does not work, so a faux, or timid, attempt to incorporate conservatism into a progressive program, does not make sense.

One argument remained for the political right, even after their victory in 2016, electing the outsider who had never held public office, was ignorant of history and policy, and yet was confident that "only he" could handle the presidency. In the face of his disastrous performance, conservatives could still argue that the makeup of the Court justified any Republican, however bad, over any Democrat, however "good." Well, not even the conservative, politicized, Court could satisfy. In June of 2020, the Court handed down the decision in *Bostock* v *Clayton County*. The decision provided protection for trans people specifically and many, many, others as well. The people who were delighted tended to be Democrats. Conservatives, especially the fundamentalist-evangelical wing that was so influential in the Republican Party, were outraged.

Reagan failed to satisfy his base; the Bushes disappointed; even the darling of the fundamentalist-evangelicals who ultimately (and tragically) came to the White House could not manage to accomplish what the conservatives wanted—and they certainly wanted it. Even conservatives who were sufficiently rational to recognize that their president was incompetent, arrogant, completely self-centered, and unfit for the office would be likely to say, "But the Court"!! (That was usually after they had said, "But Hillary's emails!") Well, of course the Court—in fact most of the federal judiciary—now is as thoroughly corrupted, as they want, but remember, conservatives demand 100%. They will ignore a huge trend in their favor, if a single ruling goes against their demands. Might it be appropriate to say, "their unworkable demands"?

Even Moscow Mitch's theft of a Supreme Court seat did not prevent a thumb into the eye of the bigots after they had denied President Obama his due and prevented him from filling a vacancy. When they succeeded in placing an ultra-right-wing judge on the Court, that ultimate appointee not only supported *Bostock*, guaranteeing rights for gay and trans people, but actually *wrote the majority opinion.* Conservatives found it especially galling that, in a Court dominated by the hard right, the decision was not narrow; it was six to three.

Also, in the same month as *Bostock*, the Court refused to accept a California church's nonsensical assertion that the governor's order banning large gatherings because of the coronavirus was "religious discrimination." Chief Justice Roberts explained the majority's decision in plain language, of course causing those on the right to blast him unmercifully. What was disturbing about the decision, which certainly was the correct one, was that it was only 5 to 4 when it should have been unanimous. For conservatives, though, it was heresy. Their guy had let them down. They were disappointed once more, as they continually are, regardless of their victories.

Again, in that same month, the Court overturned an administration policy because of the sloppy manner in which it had been justified. The administration had sought to cancel a program that established Deferred Action for Childhood Arrivals (DACA), begun under President Obama. The program prevents deportation of undocumented residents who arrived as children; deportation for the sole reason that they do not have adequate documentation. Remember how conservatives hate losing based on "technicalities"? They certainly don't object to *winning* no matter how, technicalities or not. Anyway, isn't it true that rulings *always* are based on technicalities—isn't that the substance of law? Once more, Chief Justice Roberts, an unabashed conservative, was in the majority. Once again, it was 5 to 4. Once again, conservatives squealed as if they had been victimized, because their efforts to create other victims had failed.

Yet, their efforts had failed in this instance only for the time being. The decision did agree that a president has the authority to cancel the program, but that it had to be done according to law—something that the administration and its supporters tended to think was unreasonable. In any case, conservatives insist on instant gratification. When they want something, they want it *now!*

This verified what I had written in 2017. It also meant I had been one of those who were correctly assessing the situation in early 2020, when I brought out *The Common Sense Manifesto.* Although *Common Sense* came out before the pandemic, its arguments not only remain valid, but are especially timely.

The ravages of the coronavirus made it clear that a different, and more realistic approach to the political economy was in order. Fortunately, many of the more enlightened members of the Democratic Party had gained insights from modern monetary theory. Taxes are important to control excesses of income inequality. At any level, they are important as regulatory measures. At the national level, however, taxes did not, and do not, fund governmental programs. Despite the universal tendency to demand caution with "The Taxpayer's Money," it is not taxpayers who pay for government activity at the national level. The national government creates the country's currency, and it pays its bills with the dollars it creates.

Creating and spending money does not reduce the national government's ability to generate more. Bringing in huge amounts of taxes does not enhance its ability to do so. Therefore, it is never appropriate when considering a program of the national government to ask "where is the money coming from? How do we pay for it?"—even though that is invariably the question opponents raise. Note that those most concerned about paying for a program tend to be those who wish to keep government powers too limited, especially with regard to tax, and too limited to place regulations on great wealth—just as ante-bellum southerners wanted to keep the national government too weak ever to interfere with their "Peculiar Institution," or to put it more precisely, to prevent wealthy southerners from buying, owning, controlling, and selling human beings—not to mention raping them.

When planning a new program, it should always be crafted to be the best program possible, without regard to cost. That was the way LBJ was able to get Medicare passed, and why it was and is, by and large, a good program despite its limitations. He ordered his aides to ignore economic forecasts, to plan for good performance, and to disregard costs. A program planned to be the least expensive will always suffer in quality. As one very wise economist, Stephanie Kelton, remarks, "anything that is technically feasible, is financially affordable." It is telling that Kelton's brilliant book, *The Deficit Myth*, almost immediately upon publication in 2020, jumped onto the best seller list of the *New York Times*.

That impressive book's launch took place in a month that was most fascinating for a number of reasons. June was the month of Supreme Court decisions restraining an administration dominated both by evil, and by incompetence. It was the month of huge demonstrations across the country that began in late May in response to the shocking and inexcusable murder of George Floyd by a Minneapolis policeman; a murder that was one of a long-time pattern of assassinations of Black Americans by police officers who abused their power because of viciousness, fear, or both. Timid cops can be as dangerous as venomous ones.

It was a month in which the public learned that the administration, an administration that openly justified violence and brutality, especially—although not exclusively—directed toward people of color, also had secretly sent drones to cities across the land to spy upon peaceful demonstrations. The administration tried, fortunately vainly, to convince the public that a left-wing group, Antifa (for "anti-fascists"), was the source of trouble, when there was almost no Antifa presence, and none that resulted in violence. The violence, as state authorities verified, tended to come from organized right-wing outsiders, many of whom sought to create a civil war. It is to be expected, though, that any group, however benign or however unorganized, could expect this president's hostility if it calls itself Anti-Fascist. How dare they?

Regarding Modern Monetary Theory, do proponents argue there are no limits? Not at all. There are limits to a sovereign government's spending power, of course, but they are very broad, and nowhere near so restrictive as conventional wisdom warns. The fear, generally irrational, is of inflation. Opponents will always thunder about its dangers, but inflation does not happen as a reaction to money creation so long as the productive capacity of the economy is adequate. The government must study inflation carefully and keep it under control. That is well within the ability of government to accomplish, assuming competent leadership.

One of Joe Biden's burdens is the mistakes that he has made throughout his career. To be fair, many Democrats have shared in those, and other, mistakes. Anita Hill is, I am sure, capable of providing expert testimony of that. One of Joe Biden's strengths, though, is his ability to recognize his mistakes, to acknowledge them, to improve, and then to proceed. His choice of Kamala Harris is evidence of that, and she will provide wise counsel. We can be relieved that Biden would never say, "Only I can fix it." "My actions are perfect." "I never make mistakes." "Only I am important."

I wasn't sure how things would go, but it was a relief to see that Biden began exactly as he should have. As a candidate, he put together a broad group of advisers to seek counsel on appointments, his vice president, and on policy. Although I didn't know it at the time, as soon as he was nominated formally, Biden also called together another substantial group of advisers—a modern version of FDR's "Brains Trust," although Biden's was much broader than FDR's. The group's breadth brought in substantial representation from people of color, including those active in Black Lives Matter, to ensure that those who had not been fully incorporated into the benefits of the political, social, and economic system would contribute substantially to new policy proposals. I found out about this specially-selected group considerably before it was publicized, because I had friends who were participants.

The group was well chosen, and quickly began a serious and thoughtful process designed to ensure not only that a Biden-Harris administration would consider all the necessary subjects, but that each one would receive full attention, and that nothing would fall by the wayside. At the outset, one key principle was accepted unanimously as among the uppermost, along with environmental concerns, and the restoration of all agencies that the 45th president had emasculated, such as the Environmental Protection Agency, and the Consumer Financial Protection Bureau: all residents should be treated with equal human dignity, regardless of race, gender, age, or social class; for everyone, there should be acceptable levels of living conditions, employment, education, health care, internet access, banking and legal services, and full accessibility to the many essential services of civilization (postal, health, social security, licensing, taxation, transportation, voting, etc.). There should also be a complete prohibition of involuntary servitude with discussion of a possible exception for national service that could include military conscription in the case of a true and verified emergency situation.

Many critics had been harsh regarding President Obama's strong emphasis on health care initially in his administration, saying he could have accomplished more if he had turned his attention first to other things. For example, during the early years of the Obama administration, I heard then Senator Evan Bayh, a conservative Democrat from Indiana, argue that Obama's push for health care had been detrimental to progressive values; that Obama should have been more moderate, in order to be able to advocate progressive measures later. In other words, to be successfully progressive, it was necessary to avoid advocating progressive measures. If that contorted reasoning ever made sense, it certainly didn't for the beginning of the Biden-Harris administration.

President Biden was in somewhat the same situation as the one in which Franklin D. Roosevelt found himself as he took office in March of 1933: there was so much that had to be done quickly to repair the chaos. In Biden's case, the chaos was created by the most destructive presidential administration in America's history, and one of the worst anywhere. Biden faced a wrecked government far more damaged than the one FDR had inherited from Hoover, exacerbated by the ravages of a pandemic that had completely overwhelmed an oblivious federal government. Hoover had never attempted deliberately to be destructive. In contrast to Biden's predecessor, Hoover was a patriot who wanted to do the best for his country—however incapable he was of doing so because of his limiting and conservative ideology.

Thus, Biden put together his highly diverse team, consisting of most of his opponents for the nomination, especially those of the top tier. Added to those were a few key representatives and senators, and a handful of governors and mayors. Also participating were some scholars and aides whom Biden had long respected. Most noteworthy were former Presidents Obama, Clinton, and Carter—three intellectual power houses, along with two more: Hillary Clinton, and Michelle Obama. Happily, he also included "The Squad," four young women of color in their first terms who had vigorously brought progressive views to the U. S. House of Representatives: Ilhan Omar of Minnesota, Ayanna Pressley of Massachusetts, Rashida Tlaib of Michigan, and "AOC," Alexandria Ocasio-Cortez of New York. Vice President Harris was of course an active participant. These women brought different backgrounds, religions, races, and constituencies to the House—so much for the nonsensical complaints about "coastal elites" vs. "the heartland"—but they had one thing very much in common: a courageous and vigorous concern for and knowledge of the issues motivated by outrage over injustice and fueled by the keenest of intellects.

Equally noteworthy were those whom Biden did not call on for advice. There was no one from Wall Street; there were no bankers, no hedge-fund billionaires, no economic advisers from previous administrations, no Republicans or anyone who had accepted the previous president without protest. People of good will should feel a long-overdue sense of relief for this. The age of neoliberalism was behind us, as was the age of conservatism.

There was also no representation from the libertarian fringe that had no sense of proportion. There was great sensitivity among all participants to the need for human freedom, but definitions are important. Trivial matters are not to be considered equivalent to those of great import. Requiring the wearing of a mask for public health purposes, for example, is hardly a major infringement on freedom, despite the bleats from some officials and others that "no government should have the right to prescribe what you wear!" That, of course, is ridiculous. No jurisdiction in the United States does, or ever has, permitted people to appear in general public places nude from the waist down, and "libertarians" have never objected to this, since their own sensibilities are involved. They become incensed only when they reject science and common sense and proclaim that they have a right to breathe indiscriminately on anyone else in public. For *real* restriction of human freedom, one need go no further than to observe the almost universal Republican attempt to suppress the ability to vote of any qualified American whom they suspect might not vote for them. Where are the libertarian objections to this true violation of civil rights?

I was happy to discover that with Biden's enthusiastic approval, his advisers turned first to FDR's proposal for an "Economic Bill of Rights." The New Deal president first outlined it to the public in his State of the Union Address of 1944 and called for it again in his final such address in 1945. The great FDR had no time to secure his plan. He died suddenly, shortly after again calling for action. It now is much past time for the country finally to turn its attention again to FDR's brilliant proposals. In fact, it's tragic that now, three-quarters of a century later, opposition to such an admirable—and absolutely affordable—plan still has kept it even from being considered, let alone being implemented. President Truman succeeded FDR, and would have implemented it, but a conservative reaction following World War Two brought Republican control to the Congress that began in January 1947.

It took all of Truman's skill to keep that Congress, so resentful of FDR, from rolling back the New Deal. There was no possibility that it would have implemented his brilliant program. And brilliant it was. This excerpt indicates clearly what FDR proposed (despite some language that would need now to be updated):

> We have come to a clear realization of the fact that true
> individual freedom cannot exist without economic se-

curity and independence. "Necessitous men are not free men." People who are hungry and out of a job are the stuff of which dictatorships are made.

In our day these economic truths have become accepted as self-evident. We have accepted, so to speak, a second Bill of Rights under which a new basis of security and prosperity can be established for all—regardless of station, race, or creed.

Among these are:

- The right to a useful and remunerative job in the industries or shops or farms or mines of the nation;

- The right to earn enough to provide adequate food and clothing and recreation;

- The right of every farmer to raise and sell his products at a return which will give him and his family a decent living;

- The right of every businessman, large and small, to trade in an atmosphere of freedom from unfair competition and domination by monopolies at home or abroad;

- The right of every family to a decent home;

- The right to adequate medical care and the opportunity to achieve and enjoy good health;

- The right to adequate protection from the economic fears of old age, sickness, accident, and unemployment;

- The right to a good education.

All of these rights spell security. And after this war is won we must be prepared to move forward, in the implementation of these rights, to new goals of human happiness and well-being.

America's own rightful place in the world depends in large part upon how fully these and similar rights have been carried into practice for our citizens.

Biden and his group studied these proposals, accepted them, and brought them up to date to meet the needs of the 21st century, including re-wording language that left out women. They added new rights, ensured that all were environmentally friendly, and added strong environmental protections. It became a modern, and much expanded, version of what The Squad and some others had been proposing as "The Green New Deal."

CHAPTER 4

POLITICAL EQUALITY AND FULL CIVIL RIGHTS FOR ALL

My discussion now will describe actual accomplishments, and also plans that are being actively implemented. Many other programs will follow, but of course, not all will materialize. Since I want to keep this as grounded as possible, I will deal only with matters completed, or underway. For those that involve constitutional amendments, I include only those for which substantial planning is already taking place.

Now is time to seriously consider constitutional amendments to remedy some of the Constitution's clear defects, and to ensure that all citizens have equal rights before the law. The Democrats had plans well formulated by the time they actually took power. These plans presupposed elimination of the electoral college. Removing it creates votes of equal power in selecting presidents, rather than votes of more or less power reflecting the location from which a vote is cast. The complaint that cities, or California, would always decide elections is foolish. For one thing, a national popular vote would count the votes of Republicans in California, as the electoral college does not. For another, the old Confederacy has far more votes than California does. In fact, their two largest states alone, Florida and Texas, together have considerably more population, and more votes, than California has. The "coasts versus 'heartland'" argument is similarly silly, for similar reasons, and it ignores the fact that there is not a sharp coast/interior split. In 2016, for example, Colorado, New Mexico, Minnesota, and Illinois voted for Hillary Clinton, and they hardly are coastal. For another, the Carolinas, Georgia, and Florida went Republican, and they clearly are coastal. Pennsylvania, Michigan, and Wisconsin are "heartland" (although Pennsylvania is almost on the east coast), but their votes for the Republican were razor thin, and they had in fact been considered (erroneously, obviously and unfortunately) to have constituted a "blue wall" that would have ensured a Democratic victory. For arguments to be taken seriously by anyone thoughtful, they should not be obvious nonsense.

Not only does a true national popular vote bring the country closer to one person one vote, it also removes any question about the power of a state's legislature to supersede the popular vote within that state. In the July 2020 *Chiafalo v. Washington* decision asserting that, "Long settled and established practices may have great weight," and that there is a "longstanding tradition in which electors ... are to vote for the candidate whom the State's voters have chosen," the Supreme Court seems clearly to have asserted a right of the people to vote for presidential electors.

On the other hand, the Supreme Court held, in *Bush* v. *Gore* that any state legislature at any time in the process, even after the people have voted, has the power to override their will and substitute the legislators' should it choose to do so. *Chiafalo* seems to have overruled this provision of *Bush* v. *Gore*, but a constitutional amendment eliminating the electoral college and substituting the popular vote would clear up any possible ambiguity, or the possibility of another Court decision that might incorporate different reasoning.

Without the electoral college, no longer would there be the possibility of the House of Representatives choosing a president based upon the judgment of state delegations, in which each state has only a single vote. Under the electoral college, when the House selects a president, Alaska with roughly 784,000 residents, has the same influence as Texas has, even though Texas has about 29,000,000 residents. That isn't even the greatest extreme. California has a population more than 10 million greater than that of Texas, and even it would be reduced in voting power to be the equal of, say, Wyoming, with about 567,000 residents, which makes it smaller in population than Alaska.

Eliminating the electoral college would have another effect, making it easier to admit the District of Columbia to the Union as a state without the awkwardness that the 23rd Amendment would create. The 23rd Amendment provides residents of the District with presidential electors, not to exceed those assigned to the smallest state, which is three. Without the electoral college, Congress could legislate the seat of government to be merely the few blocks with the White House, the Capitol, and the Supreme Court to be the "seat of government," freeing the rest of the District to be the state; and without the electoral college those few blocks would not have to be assigned electoral votes.

The House of Representatives on June 29, 2020 did vote on a statehood bill for the District to be admitted to the Union as a new state, Washington, Douglass Commonwealth (renaming the District of Columbia for the great orator and anti-slavery activist who himself had escaped from slavery, Frederick Douglass). The bill was appropriately numbered H.R. 51 and called for an expedited repeal of the 23rd Amendment upon statehood, which any amendment eliminating the electoral college would no doubt have included at any rate. Of course, no Republican voted in favor, nor did the Republican Senate even act on it. Had they taken it up and by some miracle passed the bill, the Republican president vowed to veto it, saying that Democrats only wanted more Democratic members of Congress. Mitch McConnell, the Senate Republican leader, said (with characteristic irrationality) that the movements for statehood for D. C. and Puerto Rico were moves toward "socialism" (defined, no doubt, as anything other than Republican orthodoxy).

If D.C. were admitted as a state, it would not be the smallest by population; it would be larger than Wyoming and Vermont. Puerto Rico already has many attributes of a state, and justice indicates that it should be admitted to the Union also (presuming that its population favors admission). It would be far larger than the smallest states and would rank with six other states that have four US representatives each, thus with six electoral votes (until, with luck, the electoral college is relegated to history's dumpster).

The blue tsunami also had made it possible to attack political inequality on many fronts, and the victorious Democrats set about immediately to do so. They quickly made election day a national holiday, and required ample, accessible, polling places and national voter registration for all citizens of voting age. They banned all requirements calculated to present obstacles to voting, such as notarized ballots or presentation of ID. That thwarted the prevailing GOP practice of suppressing any votes the Republicans deemed unlikely to favor them. Electoral boundaries in every state would be subjected to national review for fairness. In addition, they made any attempts at voter suppression a federal felony; voter fraud, if it clearly and deliberately existed, would be a misdemeanor, with no enormous penalty such as multi-year prison time. With a major boost from the coronavirus pandemic, they made voting by mail possible for anyone who chooses not to vote in person. Of course, that required that the Postal Service be fully supported by the government, and that the ridiculous restrictions it had to endure since 2007 from the so-called Postal Accountability and Enhancement Act be removed. The Democrats accomplished that immediately, to be effective while they planned for a renewed Post Office Department to be responsible for providing full broadband coverage to every household in the United States, with effective security. I will discuss that later.

An updated version of the Fairness Doctrine also was on the agenda, to ensure that various political opinions would be represented fairly, and that no use of the airways, cable, or other electronic medium could be used purely for political propaganda—or be infected by foreign propaganda. This would not ban domestic political propaganda from broadcasting but would ensure that it would be offset by a diversity of views.

The conventional wisdom that the right wing had crafted skillfully, had carefully incorporated the assumption that a fairness doctrine cannot operate in a manner consistent with the First Amendment, especially in view of the multiplicity of sources in the modern world of communication. Thus, the argument went, there could be no attempt to ensure a reasonable degree of fairness. That puts it boldly, and the conservatives had been nothing if not bold in their assertions. Nevertheless, some sort of fairness doctrine had been in effect for decades since the Radio Act of 1927, which regulated the limited airways, and required broadcasting to operate in the public interest. The Federal Communication Commission mandated in 1949 that broadcasters include matters of public interest in their programming, and that they operate fairly.

In 1987, though, as the Reagan Revolution was clamping its jaws ever more deeply on American policies, Reagan's Federal Communications Commission eliminated the doctrine. Congress quickly passed an act mandating fairness, but Reagan vetoed it, and Republicans applauded, assuming no doubt correctly that fairness is explicitly liberal (as Steven Colbert, in his former guise, put it in his immortal comment: "reality has a well-known liberal bias").

That bit of Reaganite mischief now is little remembered, but anyone concerned about the character of talk radio, Fox News as an arm of Republican orthodoxy (or as often as not, its driver), and the currently warped character of public discourse should think of Reagan as the godfather—in more ways than one. Even a cursory look at radio and television station ownership reveals a huge concentration, with the market dominated by a handful of companies. In a most sinister manner, those companies tend to be highly conservative, and rigidly control the broadcasting content over which they have power. Certainly, a fairness doctrine would be considerably more difficult to devise while maintaining freedom of speech than it was during times with limited media available, but the planners were confident that they could accomplish it.

As a part of the policy package to provide greater equality, the Democrats increased the size of the U. S. House. When the first Congress proposed the Bill of Rights, it contained two proposed amendments that lacked ratification by the requisite three-fourths of the states. One ultimately became the 27th Amendment, securing ratification some two centuries later, in 1992. That reflected the huge suspicion of congressional salaries that has never abated. Few things create greater anger among the people than members of Congress raising their salaries (it's odd that the previous president directing business his way, thus lining his pockets, generated no concern among Republicans). The Amendment stipulates that any congressional salary increase cannot take effect until after the election following the enactment of the law increasing the salaries.

The other proposed amendment has never been ratified. It called for the U. S. House to have a representative for each 30,000 residents, increasing as population increased until it would have been one for every 50,000. Until 1911, the House kept roughly consistent in size with the size of the U.S. population. Since then, however, until the recent changes, legislation capped it at 435 (except temporarily for two years that had an extra member for each of the newly-admitted states of Alaska, and then Hawaii). When the size of the House was capped at 435, the average congressional district had about three-quarters of a million residents.

There were two primary disadvantages of these huge districts. They made for very expensive campaigns, and they tended to absorb minorities into larger districts in which they had little influence. Thus, they increased the influence of money in politics, and they reduced actual representation. Since the smallest states must have at least one representative, the 435 cap created anomalies such as Wyoming with a representative for fewer than 600,000 residents, while Montana, with about a million residents also had only one. Rhode Island, which has about the same population as Montana, had two.

The Democrats thus moved quickly and increased the size of the House. Although the politics might have presented difficulties, the Constitution did not. A simple law increasing the House's size was all that was required. They tripled the membership and provided for at least two representatives for the smallest states. With each state having at least two congressional districts, the average district size across the country became about a quarter million. That is far closer to the size that Madison favored in his proposed, but ill-fated, amendment. As for logistics, since the capitol is too small to accommodate such a huge House, the legislation called for a new building to do so. The building is nearing completion as I write. We're planning a visit to Washington soon, and look forward to seeing the new structure. I'm afraid we still will have to have masks, hand sanitizer, and all the rest of the things we need to keep heathy. These conditions may last for our lifetimes, but I hope not for yours.

Equal rights before the law became the heart of the Democrats' plans, including, in addition to the measures I have already mentioned, the following already underway: restructuring of the tax system to reduce sharply the extent of income inequality, and ultimately to make it impossible to be a billionaire; sharp increase of the minimum wage; judicial restructuring, along with legislative support making it clear that the interests of the people take precedence to the interests of wealth, and specifying that spending is not speech, nor do corporations have the rights of people; government as the employer of last resort; free higher education at public institutions, with adequate support of those institutions; free child care and kindergarten for children from age 3 to the first grade; banning of private prisons nationwide and all such delegation of government authority to private for-profit businesses, and a national ombudsman to ensure that residents do not suffer from unfair practices, law enforcement brutality, sexual, gender, or racial discrimination, or forced labor (I'll refer again to this later). Also, that equal rights are enforced for all. This specifically includes a comprehensive immigration plan. That provides for humane treatment, for the welcoming of those fleeing oppression and brutality, and for a regular path to citizenship. All these things together became a new version of FDR's Economic Bill of Rights, which includes universal health care. These are under the form of a Green New Deal with a Green Great Society. I shall describe them in greater detail.

CHAPTER 5

THE INFRASTRUCTURE

New Year's Day 2022

Even if the pandemic were not inhibiting revelry, I am not a night owl, and would not have stayed up to welcome the New Year. I got up bright and early this morning, with no hangover or sleep deprivation to tempt me to skip my labors—and writing, indeed, is labor. It brings a sense of accomplishment, though, and I hope it will help you and others in years to come to have a better understanding of what took place, and how a strong reaction brought about correction, even reform that had been needed long before the election of a president who made a bull in a China shop appear moderate by contrast.

In any case, I forgot one thing: Happy New Year!

As I continue with this record drawn from my journal, I am calling this chapter The Infrastructure, but what I'm doing consists of two parts. My non-traditional use of the term describes the foundation of the progressive programs the Democrats established in 2021. The second part describes expansion of the systems and physical structures constituting what most people understand as infrastructure.

Regardless of any other consideration, it was essential for the new government, under complete control of Democrats, to move quickly and effectively to reform the entire political system. Happily, they wasted no time, and moved as vigorously as FDR did when he took office in March of 1933 (after that, the new 20th Amendment changed the inaugural date to January 20th). As heralded as America's political system has been, and much of the praise has been absolutely justified, it is not and never has been perfect.

Racism is America's original sin. It was present at the founding, and already had dominated for centuries at the time of the Constitution. It led to the Civil War of course. Republicans have tended to treat racism and poverty the same. If they haven't been poor (and sometimes, even if they have), they refuse to admit the reality of poverty, and therefore its effects. If they haven't suffered the effects of racism, it must not exist, and therefore it has no ill effects. This denial can even undergird an absurd Supreme Court decision (*Shelby County* v. *Holder, 2013*), gutting the Voting Rights Act because racism, the conservative justices in the majority said with a straight face, no longer is a problem. How blind must one be to believe that? It takes no great perception to understand that racism is the country's original sin and that it remains a pernicious influence throughout society and politics.

That sin and all vestiges of it must be purged, and President Biden is in a position to ensure fundamental change. Although he is not the dynamic figure, eager to right all wrongs, that Lyndon B. Johnson was, Biden has come around, and aided by his energetic vice president, Kamala Harris, has become a vigorous reformer. He certainly has moved in LBJ's direction—and I intend that as high praise. It was similar to what the Lincoln government managed to do, in addition to emancipation and despite the war, after southerners had departed Congress to return to their southern homes and attempt in earnest to subvert the Constitution. In 1861, Lincoln signed into law the first income tax in American history. This was well before the 16th Amendment, of course. In 1862, Lincoln signed the Homestead Act . In addition, he also signed the Morrill Act that greatly expanded higher education and made it more accessible (this created land-grant colleges that have evolved into the great, often world-class, land-grant universities). He also signed an act creating the Department of Agriculture, which began national programs of conservation, in addition to fostering agriculture. Although it's less widely known he signed the Yosemite Grant Act that foreshadowed the American system of national parks that was to begin under President Grant with the formation of Yellowstone. Later that same year he signed an act encouraging the construction of railroads and telegraph lines to unite east and west. The next two years he signed into law acts creating a national currency and a mechanism for national control of banks. Much of this program, unfortunately, fit into the American pattern of oppressing the native population and seizing their land.

Taking Injustice Seriously

Happily—especially since the outrage following the unspeakable murders of Black people by agents of the state, that is by police, the Biden-Harris administration was far more aware of, and conscious of the need for, considering the welfare of all segments of American society than was typical in the nineteenth century, or even much of the time before him, up to and including the first two decades of our current century—especially the four years immediately before he took office. The proliferation of murders by police, and brutalization of African-American communities makes obvious the need to strike out vigorously against injustice.

It may be impossible to eliminate all injustice—nothing in this vale of tears is perfect—but it is the obligation of a decent political system to do everything possible to ensure fair treatment. There are indications as far back as ancient China provisions existed to deal with unjust treatment by government officials. In early modern times, to perform that duty, an office of the *Ombudsman* (from the Swedish) developed in Scandinavia.

President Biden's advisers recommended, the creation of a new agency to perform *ombudsman* functions, and he accepted quickly, and gladly.

The vice president, by statute, was made the agency's head, and Vice President Harris moved quickly to implement its function: to investigate *thoroughly and objectively* any instances of mistreatment of anyone in the country by any government official, national, state, or local. That definitely includes acts of police brutality. She certainly did not have to be convinced that Black Lives Matter. As a former prosecutor and California's attorney general, she knew precisely what to do in that regard. Her function also includes dealing with instances of arbitrary, unjust, or illegal treatment anywhere in the political system of anyone, irrespective of citizenship or legal status. The agency has full legal authority, is required by law to be fully staffed and operational at all times and can levy penalties or bring prosecutions before a federal court. If circumstances warrant, it can even correct injustices that were fully legal, but nevertheless unfair.

To make sure it protects rights fully, the Ombudsman officers and staff are assigned to function parallel with U.S. district courts and are accessible to every resident. They function with the strong assistance of advisory groups formed by the communities within which they operate, and which are affected by adverse discrimination. Even skeptical observers have already been astonished at the effectiveness of the new *ombudsman* function under the extraordinary leadership of Vice President Harris.

Ensuring the Right to Vote

The most urgent reform, fundamental to everything else, was the overhaul of the country's voting system I described earlier, to ensure that all citizens of voting age find it simple and easy to cast their votes. For this to take place, it was necessary to recognize the extent of Republican policies and practices of voter suppression, and to counter them. That was best done by ensuring uniform procedures across the country, by eliminating harsh penalties for casting an ineligible vote, by requiring ample polling places, and by eliminating as many obstacles as possible. Thus, voter registration became national, district boundaries had to be approved by national judicial authorities to ensure fairness and eliminate gerrymandering.

Eliminating the Department of Homeland Security: Protecting Civil Liberties

Among the most important reforms that President Biden had to work on immediately was elimination of the ill-conceived Department of Homeland Security. The need became clear when Biden's unlamented predecessor in July of 2020 unleashed completely militarized troops on the people of Portland, Oregon and then elsewhere for completely transparent political purposes. He sought primarily to generate photos and videos to be used in his re-election campaign. Despite scenes reminiscent of the early days of Nazi Germany, some of the photos that were released to foster his campaign showed images of street violence that had taken places years before in Ukraine!

The one silver lining of the terrorist imposition of federal storm troopers upon peaceful civilian protestors is that it made it clear to all who were not blinded by ideology (or deplorable prejudice) that fascism, or something similar to fascism, was a possibility in the United States, despite our constitutional safeguards and our traditions of the rule of law. A president has enormous power, but Congress can provide a check, as to some extent can the attorney general. Unfortunately, if an attorney general disregards the good of the country and instead functions as the president's agent, there can be no check from the Department of Justice. Even more important, if the president's party functions as a personal guard, or is uninterested in good government as opposed to protecting its hold on the White House, and if that party controls either House or Senate, the most powerful potential check on a president's power becomes ineffective.

Before the violence that the 45th president gleefully unleashed in Portland on American citizens who were exercising their constitutional right to protest, it was routinely condemned as beyond the pale to compare authoritarian actions by those in power in the United States with Germany's Nazis. However harsh American conservatives were, they were never to be compared to the Third Reich; to do so was bad form, and uncalled for. The argument was well-crafted to protect conservative administrations. Then, came a secretary of Homeland Security (an acting secretary) to proclaim the need for "proactive" arrests. By definition, that involves seizing people for acts they have not committed. That secretary, certainly, was exercising power not envisioned by the Founders. Moreover, since he was merely "acting," and not fully appointed, he had not had confirmation by the Senate. The sitting president, while always reluctant to fill many, many, positions throughout government, had developed the habit of putting "acting" officials into top positions to give himself more flexibility in directing—and firing—them whenever the whim stuck him.

Suddenly, the similarity of the American right with its German predecessors became too obvious to ignore. Comparisons began to creep into press coverage without the pious, pearl-clutching, protests that not long before they would have occasioned. The president's earlier "good people on both sides," reference to neo-Nazis in Charlottesville, when one of their deranged goons drove at high speed into a crowd killing a young woman, was a promise of what was to come; and come inevitably it did.

Viewing federal agents in full battle gear gassing and clubbing citizens on the street over the protests of Portland's mayor and Oregon's governor was reminiscent of scenes in Germany in the early 1930s. The difference was that the Germans, with Hitler's fascination with symbolism, displayed banners, swastikas, and other accouterments of Nazi tyranny. Those in America, acting as the personal agents of the president and his henchmen heading DHS and the Department of Justice, were secretive, and wore nothing official at all. Without displaying any identification, they beat people unmercifully, kidnapped Americans off the sidewalks and threw them into unmarked, but highly sinister vans, and drove them off to unknown destinations. Regardless of whether the victims had any way of knowing that the thuggish treatment they were receiving came from officials, any attempt at fighting back—at self-defense—was clearly evidence of "resisting arrest," or of using violence against an agent of the law. The president was so pleased with the chaos he created that he warned other American cities to expect the same.

The misuse of immigration demonstrated the danger to the American people, and to civilian rule, of the huge department. It had to go. Former Senator Barbara Boxer, in lamenting her vote in 2002 to authorize creation of the new department, said she had been wrong to do so. She told the *Washington Post* on July 25, 2020, that she had never imagined that an American president would use "unconfirmed puppets like acting DHS secretary Chad Wolf and his deputy Ken Cuccinelli, to terrorize our own citizens in our own country." The goal in creating the department, she said, had been to protect our people, not to hurt them; not to cause harm. Sadly, she noted, the act creating the department had no built-in protection "to stop a power-hungry president from misusing a powerful federal police force, hidden in disparate agencies, controlled by one agency head." Nor could she have envisioned the institutionalized cruelty that was incorporated deliberately into our national policy.

Biden quickly secured legislation to transfer components such as the Secret Service back to the Treasury Department, and the Coast Guard back to the Department of Transportation, from which they had been plucked in the early years of George W. Bush's administration. FEMA, the Federal Emergency Management Administration, became again an independent agency reporting directly to the president, with a renewed primary mission of responding to pandemics and natural disasters, instead of devoting nearly all its resources to the effects of possible terrorist attacks. The pandemic should have made the importance of FEMA in combatting epidemics apparent to any observer, but the previous administration, having no faith in government and in any case not being interested, remained oblivious.

The Transportation Security Administration (TSA) also again became part of the Department of Transportation. Customs and Border Protection was reformed and Immigration and Customs Enforcement (ICE) was replaced by a new agency which has police functions minimized. Immigration and customs responsibilities again were placed in the Department of Justice (which itself was reformed, because of the misuse and damage that had occurred under Attorney General William "Henchman" Barr). The remaining Homeland Security units were absorbed by appropriate agencies.

DACA (Deferred Action for Childhood Arrivals) was an Obama administration program that protected immigrants whose parents had brought them as children to the States without conforming to official restrictions against arbitrary deportation. Those who were brought here as children became widely known as The Dreamers. The deportation record of the Obama administration was inexcusably harsh, but DACA was a rational, and humane, response to the situation facing childhood arrivals. Obama's successor, however, incorporated a brutality into his policy that made anything Obama sanctioned appear benign by contrast. Regardless of any consequences, President 45 couldn't stand to have anything remain that Obama began.

President Biden's executive order restoring DACA, and his subsequent support for immediate legislation conferring citizenship upon the Dreamers, was his first step toward a comprehensive program of immigration reform that led to amnesty for those others already here, a clear and welcoming path to citizenship for them, and a rationalized program for new admissions to the country. This instituted a humane policy.

The Biden-Harris administration and the Democrats joyfully stripped the institutional cruelty that Republicans had deliberately installed from national policy and made the United States again a beacon for the world. This replaced the country's record for the previous four years as inept and incredibly harsh, along with the record of the G.W. Bush years as a national apologist for torture as official policy—and brought it a long way toward restoring it to a position of respect among the world's nations. Other countries will understandably remain wary for a considerable period, in view of the damage that Republican rule left as its legacy.

Discarding the "Night Landing" Policy

At the risk of being tedious, I stress once again two factors that American reformers had to recognize, and with which they began to deal forcefully:

- The country for far too long had ignored racism, denying it exists. Ignoring it does not make it go away, and makes it unlikely, if not impossible, to remedy.

71

- The country for far too long had ignored poverty, denying it exists. Ignoring it does not make it go away, and makes it unlikely, if not impossible, to remedy.

The 45th president appeared to believe in the "magic of ignorance." Covid-19 cases increased in number because of increased testing, he said. Under his watch, the United States of America that long had prided itself on being the best at everything, suddenly became the world's basket case in handling the pandemic. Far from being seen as the best, the USA rapidly degenerated into an object of pity because of its incompetent president, protected by his party that worked to ensure he would be free to follow his idiot instincts. And, follow them he did, braying nonsensically that China had "unleashed" the virus on the US, appearing to believe that blaming China is sufficient without a comprehensive plan to handle the pandemic domestically.

The former president of the United States thus become, by impartial measure the world's worst leader, most notably in handling, or failing to handle, the coronavirus pandemic. Given his clear record, it was considerate of the world not to preempt his racist label, The China Virus, with another: The American Virus.

That president went beyond the cynical policy of distorting data to make reality seem more acceptable. Strangely, he seemed actually to believe that if cases of viral infection are not discovered, not uncovered, they literally are not and cannot be there. Discovering more cases through testing means that we should not be testing. His approach was reminiscent of the pilot's joke about nighttime engine trouble. Flying at night is considerably different from flying in daylight. If one is flying at night and the engine fails, the procedure (assuming that no landing field is within gliding distance, and the engine cannot be re-started) is to look for a dark patch, no street lights, or other indication of buildings, etc., and hope that it is not a body of water. Then the pilot glides to the area and sets the plane up for landing. Using the plane's landing lights will indicate whether the area is acceptable. If it is, the pilot lands. If not, the pilot turns off the landing light. Refusing to test is akin to turning off the landing light because you don't like what you see. It does not change reality.

The trouble is, the result of following a delusion or ignoring reality is a crash, just as the country crashed because of a president who had no idea what he was doing, and fundamentally did not even care, if only he could be made to look good.

The new Biden-Harris Democratic administration determined to do what any rational administration would do. It actually has proceeded with good-faith attempts to identify unacceptable circumstances, and then to take all feasible measures to make them as acceptable as it is possible to make them.

The Belated Re-Building of the United States

Some years ago, an American returned from China where he had observed the Olympics. I heard him interviewed on radio, and he was amazed by a high-speed rail journey he undertook there. The ride was smooth, quiet, and the train exceeded 200 mph.

Returning to the States, and arriving in Los Angeles, he embarked upon a rail journey that he said bounced noisily along at no more than 50 mph on old tracks laid on a century-old rail bed. He wondered, he said, whether he had left a modern country and returned home to the third world. China, incidentally, now has a vastly faster and technologically far more advanced train that levitates magnetically.

These are many examples of infrastructure failure: primitive transportation relying far too much on the automobile and airplane; utility-delivery systems that are inadequately protected;

and half-hearted attempts at energy saving, if that. Worse than any of these examples, though, was the horror of Flint, Michigan, where a Republican state administration usurped local authority (as it tended to do to jurisdictions with large Black populations), and to save money, without caring about any other effect of what it was doing, shifted the city's water supply to one that poisoned its population.

Much of this, like our poorly-financed public schools and universities, pothole-pocked streets and inadequate mass transit, reflects decades of conservative attacks on government services and on the very idea of taxation, especially on those of upper incomes. It also should be equally obvious that the target population that the Republican policy shift so disdained, was largely African-American. Racism no longer exists?

The Biden-Harris administration recognized the manufactured hostility toward taxation, and therefore avoided requiring any requirement that the states provide funding. It embarked upon a completely federal program of infrastructure modernization that did not require taxes to finance. The only burden on states was the need for them to provide rights-of-way when required, to be funded nationally.

Underway now across the country—all being built by union labor, and utilizing clean energy when at all possible—are projects to ensure clean and wholesome drinking water to all, effective and environmentally-friendly solid and hazardous waste handling, construction of light rail in the cities and high-speed rail throughout the land, and green energy generation ultimately to replace all fossil fuel or nuclear sources. Programs designed to reduce automobile usage combine with upgrades of streets, highways, and bridges. Tunnels, dams, and ports are being brought up to state-of-the-art standards, as are sewage-treatment facilities. It will be some time before these projects are completed, but they are coming along more quickly than anyone had expected. The Biden-Harris administration is making maximum effort to achieve reform as soon as feasible.

The government, recognizing the need for a high minimum wage sufficient for a worker with a full-time schedule to support a family of four above a realistically-calculated poverty line, now is taking a lesson from the New Deal. It is working to provide full employment, by guaranteeing a job, with benefits and adequate pay, to anyone who wishes. There is renewed recognition of the needs of America's rural population. The Department of Housing and Urban Development has existed since LBJ's administration, but there was no comparable department dealing with America's vast rural areas. Accordingly, Biden secured legislation to expand the Department of Agriculture into a Department of Agriculture and Rural Development. This new segment of the Department includes emphasis on housing, broadband connections, and health care providers. In the material from my journal's following segments, I will discuss these in some detail.

CHAPTER 6

HEALTH AND SOCIAL SECURITY FOR ALL

Health Security

Perhaps I was an unusual kid. For a time, when I was growing up I thought of the Public Health Service when my friends were romanticizing the armed forces. I knew a little about USPHS, although nothing in depth. I probably had been influenced by tales of valiant officers battling yellow fever during construction of the Panama Canal, or something such as that. Oddly, though, I never did consider a career in medicine or a related field, but I always maintained a respect for the service.

As a young adult, I was pleased and felt vindicated when the Surgeon General issued his pronouncement against smoking. When I was young, nearly everyone smoked, including most of the people I knew and my parents (who both ultimately died of tobacco-related causes). Despite the heavy, false advertising, along with the scarcity of publicized scientific information before the surgeon general's report, popular culture recognized smoking's danger. There were good reasons that "coffin nails" was a slang term for cigarettes. Yet, at the time, I was almost alone in having never been a smoker. I certainly welcomed the Surgeon General's official condemnation of smoking, but the government sent mixed messages. Congress maintained subsidies to tobacco growers, and the Commerce Department encouraged sale of American tobacco abroad, hence contributing to continued smoking elsewhere.

Gradually, the science was so compelling that tobacco use came to be seen as what it was: an addiction that created fortunes for the companies that sold it, very much to the detriment of its deliberately addicted customers. It was some time, though, before the campaign against smoking finally became effective. Now, smoking is more or less socially unacceptable, and we can all breathe easier, quite literally (that's because of government regulation. Contrary to the former president, I say three cheers for regulation!).

In the early 1960s I commuted daily for nearly a year and a half by train from Baltimore to my position in middle management with the government in Washington, D.C. The rail cars were conspicuously designated "NO SMOKING." They also were conspicuously full of cigarette smoke. Conductors contributed to the pollution by walking through the no smoking cars carrying lighted cigarettes. I have no way of knowing if any others were as offended as I was.

When the government in the early 1970s first mandated no smoking sections on passenger planes (a practice that some comedian termed similar to a "no peeing section in a swimming pool"), I remember once picking a seat (this was before assigned seating), asking the flight attendant if I were in the no-smoking section, and being told, "yes, but it's OK if you want to go ahead and smoke ..."

Later, in 1978, I was on the old Pan Am Flight 001 to Asia (in those romantic days of flying Pan Am 001 was a regular around the world flight leaving westward; Pan Am 002 was the counterpart, going around the world leaving eastward). I complained about the smoke-filled cabin that included smokers sitting in the so-called no-smoking section, only to be told that on that route to Japan, so many passengers were Japanese, and Japanese were such heavy smokers, that the airline decided not to enforce the rule. Happily—and healthily—those days are gone.

As for the Public Health Service, contrary to popular opinion its chief officer now is not the Surgeon General. The Assistant Secretary for Health (ASH) heads the USPHS, which today includes several agencies including the Food and Drug Administration, the Center for Disease Control and the National Institutes of Health. The broader Public Health Service is a part of the Department of Health and Human Services. What the public is likely to think of as the PHS (if it thinks of it at all) is The Commissioned Corps. Along with the military, the Corps is a uniformed service, one of only two non-military uniformed services of the United States. The other is the National Oceanic and Atmospheric Administration.

Officers of The Commissioned Corps wear the same uniform as the Navy and hold naval ranks (if assigned to the Coast Guard, a Commissioned Corps officer wears instead the uniform of that service—ranks are identical in both services). The Commissioned Corps is a unit of the PHS, and the Surgeon General heads the Corps, with the rank of vice admiral (three stars). The Surgeon General reports to the Assistant Secretary of Health, who, with four stars, holds the rank of admiral (and of course the assistant secretary reports to the secretary of health and human services). The Surgeon General is the public face of the Commissioned Corps, and also speaks for the Public Health Service in presenting scientific information to the public. Over time, their role became less directly involved in providing health.

As I recorded in The Journal, the Biden-Harris administration took the position that the coronavirus pandemic demanded an expanded and more vigorous role for Commissioned Corps, with a considerably greater and directly active role once more for the Surgeon General. The administration thus moved to enlarge the Corps and expand its mission. It continues to provide public health officers to other services, but now it is beginning to operate a vast new network of USPHS hospitals through the United States, all linked together to provide telemedicine, and all with their own ambulance and helicopter service available

24/7 to bring patients to the hospital when appropriate. The goal is to have adequate health facilities available to everyone in the United States, urban, rural, or quite isolated. As I discuss later, this is being accomplished through close cooperation with what had been the Postal Service, now greatly expanded and restored as a Cabinet department devoted to public service, and no longer expected to function as a "business."

Perhaps most important of all, the United States had no overall public health policy; no coordinating plan for the country. That lack was on display for all informed persons to recognize and lament, particularly when the deadly pandemic struck at a time when the vital leadership role of president of the United States was filled by an incompetent, completely uninformed, uninterested figure of colossal ignorance who nevertheless was deluded into thinking he possessed unparalleled wisdom. Thus, the need was clear when a new, capable, president took office. Quickly, the Corps under the Surgeon General was given the resources and made responsible for working with all relevant government programs, and for coming up with a comprehensive public health plan for the United States.

One of the great inadequacies of healthcare delivery in the US has been the lack of accessible health facilities in many rural areas. Under the administration's program, virtually all residents in the United States will soon be near enough to a Public Health Service hospital, to receive care—if they choose to do so—from a health practitioner regularly by telemedicine, and personally whenever required. For maximum efficiency, private facilities will be connected to the health network also.

As indicated, this vast new array of healthcare facilities required more emphasis upon and a considerable expansion of what had been the Postal Service. This is essential for delivery of medical materials, pharmaceuticals, samples for lab tests, and other items necessary for health care. When President Biden secured legislation returning the Post Office to the cabinet, it became the Department of the Post Office, Financial, and Communication Services. As such, it was freed from the unconscionable restrictions imposed by the 2006 Republican law. That law not only required a government function to perform as a business, instead of as a public service, but it greatly restricted the Postal Service's permitted activities, made it contribute to the Treasury as if it were required to pay income tax, and required it—uniquely—to prepay health and retirement benefits of its employees for fifty years.

The Veterans Health Administration has been expanded similarly. It now works closely with the Corps, and participates fully with the planning for, and implementation of, a comprehensive plan for public health for the United States, including territories, and cooperation with other countries.

The immediate objections of course were that all this would be too expensive. The rejoinder was that the United States clearly has the resources to provide whatever service is needed, and that providing health care to Americans is no less important than protecting them with military forces. Budget hawks should be reminded that, regarding the military, cost has rarely been a consideration. Funding the military may have generated complaints, but it has never caused significant reform, nor has it caused the powerful American economy to crumble.

All of this new medical infrastructure was related to the adoption of universal health care. Medicare for All was rational and an attractive idea. A too-little recognized difficulty, though, was that if not done properly, it would be a foot-in-the door for privatization. That would have been deadly for healthcare overall. For example, too much of Medicare already is provided through Part C, or "Medicare Advantage." Although Part C can provide greater benefits, it also subjects patients again to the mercy of commercial interests, which can refuse to pay claims, can drop patients, or impose restrictions that are banned from traditional Medicare. Contrary to the publicity when it was adopted, it was not a step toward greater efficiency. Rather, it is and has always been far more expensive. It provides less care per dollar received than traditional Medicare does. The reason it is tolerated is that conservatives hope that it someday may supersede traditional Medicare and be shunted off completely to the private sector.

The extra cost of Medicare Advantage should have been expected, because in the American system, private care is almost always for profit, which drains money away from providing care, to investors. Also, private systems pay astronomical salaries to executives and spend heavily on advertising, unlike government services.

Medicare for All could work well if it avoids privatization, lowers or eliminates fees, and broadens benefits as Senator Bernie Sanders and others had proposed during the campaign. Medicaid for all, however, might have presented a stronger case. Medicaid is a federal-state program. It would have to be made fully federal, with no costs to the state to work as a universal program, because states could not afford the cost. The federal government already pays 90% of the additional cost when states expand Medicaid under the Affordable Care Act. Even so, a few states, all controlled by Republicans, have refused to expand the program.

Their rationale officially is the cost; in reality, they refuse to expand it for reasons of pure ideology—it would be part of Obamacare, they so dread. Nevertheless, it is clearly irrational to refuse expansion when states are so stressed financially because their taxes are low, that even many Republican states have expanded the system, and some other very conservative

Republican states have had public referenda that have led to expansion even though their leaders oppose it.

In Maine, the archconservative, highly ideological, rigidly irrational, and not terribly bright former governor Paul LePage refused to expand Medicaid even though the public voted affirmatively. LePage added work requirements to the existing program. He soon left the governorship because of term limits; when he came to the end of his second term, his replacement, Democrat Janet Mills, removed the work requirement, expanded the program, and brought Maine into the 21st century. This was fortunate for Maine, and even for LePage, who did not have to fight a lawsuit forcing him to follow the will of the people (something many Republicans shudder about when faced with an active population).

Ironically, states that have expanded Medicaid under Obamacare, found that their overall healthcare costs declined. Not only did the federal government pay almost all the cost, but states find that expansion permitted them to spend less on many other programs, and thus operate more efficiently. In addition, their populations tended to be healthier when they had health care available. Arkansas, for example, discovered that their overall healthcare costs declined so much that they could lower their state income tax. One would think that this might have appealed to tax-hating Republicans, even if they had to use Obamacare to accomplish it, but it was not enough to convince Republican officials in states such as Kansas and Missouri that expansion would be a good idea. In Missouri, which has provisions for popular initiatives, the people forced Medicaid expansion onto the ballot, and amended the state's constitution to protect the expanded Medicaid program.

It also is ironic that the Affordable Care Act, or Obamacare, provided that all states had to expand Medicaid. Unfortunately, the ideologically biased Supreme Court struck down the requirement, creating hardships for the people of the states with Republican governments that were able somehow to convince their voters they were being protected from Obamacare's evils, such as lowering the state's overall costs, and helping more people.

Even before the Affordable Care Act, Medicaid carried a much broader range of benefits than Medicare, and had fewer or no fees, depending upon the requirements of the state involved. Although designed for the poor, Medicaid grew into a huge program for all classes short of the very wealthy. As there is no other significant program in the United States that provides long-term care (proposals for Medicare for All would have included it with the expanded benefits that had been proposed), it was left to Medicaid to cover nursing home care when needed; such care is so expensive that only the very wealthy can afford it on their own. To meet the requirements designed to benefit only the poor, though, beneficiaries who are better off must "spend down," divesting themselves of virtually all their assets before they can qualify. Fortunately, the overall control of government by progressive Democrats brought more rationality to the programs and led to universal coverage.

The actual result from the Biden-Harris administration has been a combination of Medicare and Medicaid, fully nationalized, with no fees, and a huge range of benefits including dental, auditory, and visual services, and also long-term care (with no spend-down requirement; no means test at all). Those already on Medicare were treated exactly as before, except that they have been relieved of co-pays, and now have a complete range of benefits, fully covered and paid for. No Medicare beneficiary has complained. We could not afford it Republicans said, nonsensically, since other countries with advanced economies do so, and the US is wealthier than they are.

Patients do not have to apply for the new program, and do not have to use it if they have some objection. They seek care, as they wish, and their records follow them to different facilities, if they change providers, whether by choice, or moving to another jurisdiction. The program is available to anyone who seeks service, but those who wish to remain in private care, or with private insurance, can continue to do so. For the first time in American history, anyone who wants care can get it. There are no restrictions as to networks. Any physician anywhere in the country, including territories, who accepts Medicare, or any Public Health Service facility, will provide needed care with no out-of-pocket charge to the patient.

The opposition still, says, "NO. Too expansive. Unsustainable." Of course, they always say that. Regardless, it is within the ability of the United States to provide, and now it does so. Ever since the New Deal, conservatives have been warning that we were on an unsustainable course. The result, they continue to say, will be catastrophe. Throughout some three quarters of a century, they have only become more strident. What has happened overall during that time? Catastrophe? Hardly. The United States grew ever more powerful, which should cause budget hawks to stop and think. The country still suffers from the pandemic, also, which unfortunately has not gone away as the former president and his conservative backers had insisted it would.

Undoubtedly America sustained considerable economic and health damage from the previous administration. The pandemic still is here, but at last there is a coordinated effort to deal with it. As for economic damage, common sense will suggest that whatever course America is pursuing, it is hardly "unsustainable." Maybe the pandemic and the economic breakdown, plus the huge thumping they took in the election, have made the true believers fewer and fewer. Perhaps they will shrink back into the woodwork, or otherwise cease to persuade others to follow irrational policies. One can hope.

Economic Security

In 2020, the United States was unique in that residents typically held huge personal debt related to health expenses and student loans. The healthcare delivery system generally was profit based, and more expensive than those found in other countries. Studies indicated that medical expenses overall, including time off from work, resulted in a large number of bankruptcies. The adoption of universal health care no doubt will correct that economic problem, but the effects will be felt for some time.

Also unique was the American system of higher education. As it evolved a few decades ago, a quality higher education was accessible to those of moderate income, without the need to acquire crushing debt. Most states had good universities that were affordable. Some charged little, or even no, tuition. California, for example, had a superb system free from tuition—until the governorship of Ronald Reagan led to its ruin by cutting state funding and adding tuition charges. Sadly, the Republican irrational adoption of hostility toward all taxes meant that as years passed, lower and lower percentages of the cost of higher education would be borne by the states. Had to keep those taxes down! Thus, more and more of the cost was shouldered by students and their fees, and with increasing pressure within universities to ignore all phases of academic quality except for research that brought in federal grants.

The requirement of a college degree for economic, and even social, success is now greater than ever, but costs have become outrageous, even among state supported institutions. Unfortunately, much of the financial support that had been in the form of grants became loans that had to be repaid. To make matters even worse, legislation in the 1990s made educational loans extremely difficult to discharge in bankruptcy (the result of a law signed by Bill Clinton, a Democratic president under pressure from neoliberal Democrats). Now, students and those who have co-signed for their loans have accumulated an aggregate amount of debt that far exceeds the total amount owed on credit cards or automobile loans.

It is true that there are community colleges widely available, and that they often are of quite good quality, and are relatively inexpensive. However, they normally offer only the first two years of education, so attendance at a university or a four-year college still is likely to be necessary. Only in America, have we made at least a baccalaureate education a requirement for success, while pricing it out of reach of the ordinary family without going deeply into debt, and then penalizing them further by making that debt for all practical purposes impossible to be forgiven even by bankruptcy, as other (generally far less justifiable) forms of debt can be.

That nasty situation had been engineered deliberately by decades of conservative mischief, even though it came to fruition under a president, Bill Clinton, who was not an ideologically driven conservative. Happily, though, it is now a thing of the past. The federal government under President Biden now fully funds public institutions of higher education, and there are ample grants and scholarships available to handle other expenses, such as living costs, books, computers, and other materials. Because the African-American community has faced so many extra burdens for so long, education for America's Black citizens requires special attention. Among other measures, the Democrats have followed up on a suggestion Senator Warren made during the campaign, allocating $50 billion to HBCUs (historically Black Colleges and Universities).

As for student loan debt, in the past, "quantitative easing" may have saved large corporations but no such easing was available to students, graduates, or their families. Now, the government simply has paid off all student loans. The $1.6 trillion that had accumulated was an enormous drain on the economy and on the finances of Americans. The government simply credited the amounts owed to the lenders. Was this a huge windfall to them? Yes. It might be considered collateral damage, but new, graduated income tax rates, will bring that back, and more. That tax structure now has been crafted to discourage the excesses of income inequality, and ultimately to make it no longer possible to become a billionaire. To those who might consider this to be unfair, consider just how unfair it is to permit any person to have the power—financial, political, and otherwise—that comes from having wealth that exceeds $999+ million. That amount certainly should provide anyone with every need ever desired ... except the "need" to become a billionaire. The other objection was from those who had paid off their student loans. They, too, are being compensated by tax credits, so they are getting their own windfall, and should have little if any reason to complain. The economy has benefited greatly. So has the mental health of all the middle-and low-income borrowers.

Similarly, finally rejecting decades of manufactured outrage and false charges of "unsustainability" directed at "entitlements," the Democrats have reformed Social Security. Most calls for reform have through the years been thinly disguised arguments for benefit cuts, or even for complete elimination or privatization of the system. They were ideologically, not financially, based. The new system will operate in a manner similar to the excellent—and highly successful—way it has always operated, but benefits have been greatly increased, and made even more progressive. With increases of two-to-three-fold, every beneficiary will have an increase, but those at the lower levels will have the greatest. Levels now are calculated to provide a standard of living above the poverty line for a very low-income beneficiary who has no savings and no other income.

Also directly related to other economic protections, the Biden-Harris administration moved quickly to re-energize the Consumer Financial Protection Bureau. The CFPB was the brainchild of Professor Elizabeth Warren and the result of an act signed into law by President Obama. As its acting director, Warren brought the bureau into existence and managed it superbly. For political reasons, she was not named director, so she subsequently entered politics, and now is a distinguished United States senator who was a credible contender for the Democratic presidential nomination in 2020. The Bureau under her leadership, and the leadership of its first regularly appointed director, Richard Cordray, protected consumers in numerous ways, including against predatory lending. Under the Obama administration, it returned more than $11 billion to consumers. Obama's successor, though, shared the Republican view that this was an unconscionable overreach. Such consumer protections placed unacceptable burdens upon business. The new president then fired Cordray, and the replacements effectively carried out the Republican desire to defang the bureau and undercut its mission. Biden moved quickly to clean out the employees who were sabotaging the CFPB, and restore it to its intended function, just as he did with the EPA and other agencies, which had undergone similar damage from his predecessor.

The government now is the employer of last resort, and with the infrastructure modernization throughout the country, there are ample tasks for them to tackle. The building of new healthcare facilities, alone, is an enormous undertaking. Similarly, expanding postal services is requiring new facilities across the country. Construction is thriving, along with refurbishing of some previous postal facilities that were still available after sitting unused. As with the New Deal, there also are vigorous programs for artists, musicians, writers, dramatists, all releasing additional creative energy throughout the land. Overhauling every part of the nation's basic, and aged, infrastructure is proceeding well.

One very popular program is a renewed Civilian Conservation Corps (CCC) that is a modernized version of FDR's extremely successful and popular program under the New Deal. The CCC, in its brief existence, was responsible for numerous environmental conservation projects, including planting three *billion* trees. The new CCC has adopted a similar—but much more ambitious—plan, designed by expert environmentalists, as one part of a coordinated overall environmental program.

The government will provide childcare, care for the elderly, and for others as needed. If a family member provides that care, under the new program there are stipends, and full Social Security credit for the employment.

No doubt you knew much of this already in broad outline. I hope, though, that this additional detail will help you understand just how significant these changes are, how much they were overdue, and how vital they are to the national welfare.

CHAPTER 7

THE DEPARTMENT OF THE POST OFFICE, FINANCIAL, AND COMMUNICATION SERVICES

Reviewing The Journal, I see that it hardly conveys my sense of enthusiasm. At last, America again is coming into its own. The country always contained dynamic forces, both for good and ill. Predominantly, the thrust was toward the good, but the shortcomings were so severe as to be shocking. Recently, with notable exceptions, the United States had experienced a half century or so of decline, falling behind other countries. The correction now is underway, and I hope that I now am fleshing out cold journal entries in a way that will provide again the sense of patriotic excitement that America at its best can generate.

The new Biden-Harris administration set about repairing the damage done by decades of unworkable Republican policy quite quickly, especially considering the last four years of deliberate and overt sabotage. Even many of the skeptics were amazed that the administration managed at the same time to implement astonishingly complex and urgently needed new programs.

Along with expansion of the Commissioned Corps of the Public Health Service to bolster the newly-created universal health care with a full network of public hospitals and medical facilities, the most ambitious agency enhancement by the Biden administration involves what had been the U. S. Postal Service. The postmaster general again became a major cabinet official. The new Department of the Post Office, Financial, and Communication Services represents the best of the old, and the most urgently needed of the new. In the country's earlier days, the Post Office even had an air of romance about it, and for good reason. The expansion and recreation of the Post Office

Department has recaptured some of that romance. Whether it will influence popular culture again, who knows?

The rise of newer delivery services, such as FedEx and UPS, along with the universal availability of email, texting, and related technologies have made the Post Office appear anachronistic. The reality is quite different, as events of 2020 and the absolute need for mail voting made clear. The most hardened skeptics of "snail mail" were certainly surprised, and tended to appreciate the manner in which the Postal Service was uniquely able to perform vital services to a population that largely was confined to quarters as the pandemic fastened its grip on the country. As the 2020 election loomed, much of which inevitably under the circumstances was going to have to be handled by mail, more and more of the population came to recognize that the deliberate damage that the Republican administration was continuing to inflict upon the Postal Service—after years of attempting to marginalize it—could not be tolerated; this as the president's newly-appointed postmaster general, Louis DeJoy worked vigorously to slow down and otherwise damage service. Gradually, they also became aware of how Republican policies of rigidity and austerity had created serious troubles for the agency, even before their most recent president kept ensuring that it would face many obstacles in his effort to sabotage the vote and favor his re-election. In his words, he sought to rig the process.

The Constitution specifically sanctions the post office, which existed before the Constitutional Convention. The mail service has been a part of American life before the United States existed, when the colonies still were under British control. Like most long-lived institutions, of course, it has gone through difficulties. If thoroughly understood, many of the successes of the American Post Office would be judged as dramatic. The newly-emerged country had inherited a reasonably-organized system that would become a world model. It owed much to the genius of Benjamin Franklin, who had begun as postmaster of Philadelphia in 1737 as a young man. In that position, he became familiar with local postal needs. In 1757, the British appointed him co-postmaster of the colonies, where he gained broader experience across jurisdictions. In 1775, even before the Declaration of Independence, let alone the Articles of Confederation, the Continental Congress appointed him the first postmaster for the country that was about to throw off its bonds and assert its separation from Britain. In those pre-technological days, Franklin revolutionized communication. In a mobile society such as the United States, mail has been especially important. Considering the difficulties of transportation, if there had been no mail, the many families that were dispersed would have had to accept as fact that they would lose touch forever, and likely never see, or hear from, one another again.

In today's mail system, the United States presents a fine example of egalitarianism. It treats everyone equally, regardless of social class. Whether people live in cities, suburbs, or far from an urban area is irrelevant. A letter costs the same to mail from the farthest point in the country, as it does to mail from down the street. This may help explain the hostility that many conservatives direct toward the post office. The mail is a "government service," and that always tends to offend them (unless it is a police force or the military that defends from outsiders). Also, they find few things to be so upsetting as anything that's egalitarian.

The only time they are likely to favor a sense of solidarity, "we're all in this together," is when they use it as propaganda to justify austerity programs or conscription, and try to persuade "common folk" not to misbehave, to fall in line, and to follow orders without question. Almost by definition, however much they may try to conceal it with misleading rhetoric, conservatives favor programs that protect the wealthy. They tend to do everything they can get away with to increase hardship of the disadvantaged. True national unity based on any kind of real equality is foreign to their mind set. The goal is no different, whether they are discussing expansion of Medicaid, Social Security, Medicare, public schools—or a postal system. The goal is to present obstacles to service; to have the fewest points of service possible, to close and thus reduce the number of offices, and to do whatever it takes to shift services into the private sector that they can rely on to squeeze as much money as they can from those who have little.

The less convenient government services for the general public are, they hope, the less the public will demand more, and the more often they will turn in disgust to the private sector. This is one of the major reasons for the enormous blue tsunami that turned conservatives out of office. The people finally became fed up with inadequate public services, and with the inability—or rather the unwillingness—of Republicans even to consider timely and adequate protection when a massive viral assault threatened their health and their lives.

It took truly outrageous behavior on the part of Republicans for much of the public finally to recognize that it isn't true that government is bad. Government exists to serve the people. If it governs well, the people prosper. That means it must do everything possible to provide the most services, and the best service. It also is not true, at least at the national level, that the people must pay for what it does. The national government, as I explained before, creates money. It does not have to receive taxes to pay for services, and in fact, there is no direct connection between what it spends, and what it receives in revenue.

Despite the many other services that have emerged and may continue to emerge to perform some of the same functions, the post remains vital. Only the Post Office can deliver to post office boxes. Only the post office can and will deliver to any address in the United States. It is the only relevant agency that is devoted exclusively to public service, not profit (despite Republican efforts to make it run "like a business"). It is the only agency that can deliver most first-class mail, and has a very successful package delivery service. It will inevitably be the vehicle from now on for the delivery of ballots in American elections, as it has already been for in several states for quite some time. The Post Office is the only government agency that has regular, day-to-day contact with most Americans. The letter carrier may be the only person from government that some isolated persons have contact with, and in some instances, such contact may be life-saving.

The Biden-Harris administration recognized the importance of the agency, restored it to its earlier public-service orientation, and used it as the vehicle for expanding services to the public. The new administration quickly reversed the trend of recent years that curtailed the Postal Service; a trend that had saddled it with irrational restrictions and mandated an enormous cost by requiring it to prepay retirements for decades. The House had passed such a measure lifting the harsh restrictions before the election, but the Senate, dominated by Moscow Mitch, refused to consider it. Why should the Post Office, a government agency, have to operate at a profit any more than other agencies do? No one expects the Department of Education, the U.S. Marine Corps, the F.B.I., or any other agency to "break even," let alone to show a profit. Why single out such an important service?

One of the key responsibilities assigned to the new, expanded, Post Office Department that the Biden-Harris administration is rapidly putting in place, is to implement efficient, and secure, broadband service, without charge, to every household in

America. This is especially important to rural areas and to the urban poor, and is becoming an important tool in the country's greatly improved healthcare delivery system. The new rural development authority of the Department of Agriculture has also been enormously helpful in working to develop the rural services from the newly-conceived Post Office.

With the expansion of the Commissioned Corps of the Public Health Service and its new hospital and medical facility network, the new Post Office Department will be intimately involved. It will provide connections between health facilities and households. It will ensure that each household in the country has access to smart phones and computers to make use of telemedicine. Additionally, the Department will provide helicopter services, for hospitals and also facilitate mail delivery to extremely remote areas—both when necessary for regular mail, as in cases of flood and other disaster, or to overcome extraordinary isolation—and for delivery of such things as prescription drugs and specimens for laboratory diagnosis.

The newly-incarnated post office thus is on the way to becoming the largest government agency in the United States. The Post Office Department for decades maintained a division of Postal Inspectors, who were efficient law-enforcement agents. That function continued into the Postal Service, and has been taken into the new Department and much expanded. Many of the additional duties result from including a new cybersecurity function. The cybersecurity responsibilities are designed to ensure security of all electronic transmissions in America , guarding against attacks, especially from other countries. Beyond that, the new Department is putting place a vigorous cybersecurity counter-espionage program that works in close collaboration with the FBI, the National Security Agency, the CIA, military intelligence, and other relevant agencies, private as well as public. This is not only to ensure America's security throughout its systems, but also to ensure immediate and vigorous retaliation against all attempts, foreign and domestic, to hack into American computers, public or private. This energetic and rapid response to attempts at compromising cybersecurity ensures that there will be a serious price that any group or country will have to pay for hostile behavior. It is securing our electoral systems in a manner that contrasts sharply with recent Republican attitudes toward foreign threats. At best, they dismissed them as "fake news." At worst, they actually solicited foreign involvement for political or personal reasons, and as the president did, welcomed their attacks as helpful to his campaigns. The public began to awake to the reality of this behavior as treasonous, certainly in a moral sense as unacceptable, whether or not it met the strict constitutional definition.

The remaining authority assigned to the new department makes simple banking services available to anyone in the United States, including such things as checking and savings accounts at no charge, small loans at reasonable rates, and financial counseling. Many people for various reasons—geographic isolation, lack of an address, etc.—do not have access to banking services. Middle-class people often are unaware of how difficult it is to function in a modern economy without them. Employers generally want to deposit pay directly; cashing a check is difficult and expensive; having no place to keep their income renders them vulnerable to theft and violence. Those in need of ready cash are at the mercy of a rapacious "payday loan" industry. In this, as well as in other matters, poverty brings discrimination beyond the most obvious one: lack of money. Postal banking services will remove a great obstacle in the lives of many, and there are precedents for this around the world, and even in this country.

The Postal Service offered money orders, as the Post Office did before it, and that service of course continues in the new department. Beginning in the Taft administration in 1911, Post Offices functioned as savings banks. The Postal Savings system permitted deposits that paid modest rates of interest, and were completely safe. Money deposited in a Post Office was re-deposited in local banks, thus helping the local economy. Postal Savings ended in 1967, having been determined to be no longer of importance. Now, however, circumstances have changed, and the new postal banking services perform a substantial service to society. Under the new system, Post Offices work with local credit unions, redepositing money received for savings, and therefore keep money in local communities, strengthening the people's institutions.

To summarize the new and innovative services to the public by the Department of the Post Office, Financial, and Communication Services: the Department is exercising broad new powers to ensure that every resident will have access to fundamental banking services, even in the most rural and isolated areas. Moreover, every household in the country would have full access without charge to efficient and secure broadband internet service; again, even in the most rural and isolated areas, as satellites make possible.

The Department also has a unit in every location, that is in every Post Office, that will assist residents with other government agencies, as needed and appropriate. They will help with forms of all sorts, passports, and other things that trouble many citizens. Again, service is the watchword.

Postal employees, at least those who meet the public, traditionally have worn uniforms. That made it relatively simple to convert the new Department into a new uniformed service, such as the Public Health Service's Commissioned Corps, or the National Oceanic and Atmospheric Administration (NOAA). This now is being done to recognize the Post Office's long, distinguished tradition, and to honor the vital nature of the employees' service. Departmental employees now do hold ranks, as do those in these NOAA. Most are at the enlisted level, most letter carriers, postal clerks, etc. Those with especially challenging jobs, such as dangerous routes or positions requiring highly technical skills, such as helicopter pilots and skilled cybersecurity agents, will be warrant officers, ranging from W1 to W5. Those employees at enlisted ranks with good and lengthy service exceeding twenty-five years also will be promoted to warrant officer upon retirement. This ensures a solid retirement at least at the W1 level, for any worker in the department, even those who have served at the lowest ranks, who has provided satisfactory service for a full career. Since all career employees can retire with a minimum rank of warrant officer, lifetime service with the new Post Office Department will bring a respected, and comfortable retirement, and considering the size of the Department's work force, should also help the overall economy.

Administrators, and those in certain other positions, are now to hold commissioned ranks. The postmaster general now has four stars. As a cabinet officer, and the head of an enormous agency, one holding this unique position should not be outranked by the assistant secretary for health of the Department of Health and Human Service who is an admiral (four stars), and is below cabinet rank. There is precedent for this. The Assistant Secretary for Health (ASH), immediately upon appointment becomes eligible for the rank of admiral (four stars), even with no prior uniformed service.

CHAPTER 8

REFORMING THE CORRUPTED JUDICIARY

The last really enormous change to our system that I deal with in The Journal, deals with the judiciary. As a rule, only those who are politically aware are likely to have much political knowledge beyond the headlines, and very likely even less regarding the government's judicial function.

The general public probably doesn't pay much attention to the federal courts, except when there is a sex scandal, or when we had the evil showman as president. Even sex scandals are now sufficiently normalized that they are no longer guaranteed to whip up vast waves of titillated outrage as they once would have done. This has happened, certainly, because for four years the country was coarsened by having had an abuser-in-chief sitting in the Oval Office (when he wasn't on the golf course).

One group is an exception: politically-active conservatives. The judiciary is a topic that definitely does weigh heavily on conservative minds. Evangelical-fundamentalist Republicans especially are obsessed with the courts, and seemed to think of the boisterous POTUS 45 as having been sent to them as a gift from God, despite that president's lies, personal misconduct, and subordinating the interests of the United States to hostile foreign powers. However much dissatisfaction there may be among some conservatives with some of the few more rational decisions that their recent Court appointees may have signed on to (or even written), there can be little doubt that the extreme right has had enormous success in shaping the judiciary. FDR's "Court-packing" plan was the target of great vilification from conservatives, and sometimes also from well-meaning, but naïve, figures generally supportive of the New Deal. It was an "unconstitutional attack on the Court." Well, no. There was nothing at all unconstitutional about his plan to expand the Court. Not only does the Constitution say nothing about the Court's size, that Court had gone through several expansions and contractions long before the New Deal. By no means am I a judicial specialist, but I know enough history to be aware that the Court began with only six justices (including the chief). Under President John Adams it shrank to five, but Thomas Jefferson, his successor, signed legislation raising it back to six, and later added a seventh. Under Andrew Jackson, the Court grew to nine. President Abraham Lincoln signed an act raising it to ten. After Lincoln's tragic assassination, Congress, in the Judiciary Act of 1866, shrank the Court to seven to keep Lincoln's successor, the racist Andrew Johnson, from having any appointments, preventing him from bringing a southern orientation to the tribunal.[1] In 1869, President Ulysses Grant signed legislation increasing the Court's size to nine, and it has stayed there since. Obviously, in view of all this, there is nothing sacred, or constitutionally-mandated, about its size, and nothing constitutional preventing further revisions in the number of justices.

Was FDR's proposal an attack on the Supreme Court? Of course it was, but not an unconstitutional one; the Court should be no more immune from criticism than any other political body, and it cannot help but be political. In any case, FDR's criticism did not suggest that the Court was illegitimate, nor worse yet that all judicial functions are illegitimate.

The Republican attack on the judiciary has been far stronger and more effective than FDR's would have been had it succeeded. President Roosevelt was not attempting to make the Court more ideological. It already was tilted ideologically

---

1   Note that this did not result in discharging justices. That would have been unconstitutional. The smaller size was to be achieved by not filling vacancies.

strongly to the right, and Roosevelt was merely attempting to make it more receptive to his pragmatic approach to politics. His "Court-packing" plan would simply have brought contemporary understanding onto the Court. This more recent court-packing has gone a long way toward shifting the entire judiciary toward a highly ideological orientation that is out of step not only with public preferences, but with the needs of a diverse and democratic republic in the contemporary complex, and highly technological, world. FDR was attempting to move the Court more toward public opinion; the contemporary Republican attempt has been to protect the Court (and their interests) *from* the public's will.

As an aside, one often hears condemnation of FDR's plan as going too far. FDR's second term was less successful than his first, and his scheme to pack the Court must bear some responsibility. FDR took the position, though, that he may have lost the battle, in that his plan was not enacted, but he won overall, because the Court shifted to rule in his favor. Soon, with numerous retirements of elderly justices, he had appointed a majority of the Court's members. It seems to me that FDR here has the better argument. He did get his way on policy, by and large. As for losing power in his second term, yes, but almost all presidents who serve two terms have troubles in the second. Anyone who would argue that FDR's second term would be as successful and as dramatic as his first, had he not tried to pack the Court, would be on shaky ground, indeed. His first term presents an insurmountable standard, since his accomplishments were so monumental. It would be unreasonable to expect that anyone could accomplish so much again.

The more important consideration now, though, relates to Republican judicial appointments of the last few decades. The movement to re-shape the judiciary in an ultra-conservative ideological direction began in the Ronald Reagan administration, and succeeded in moving the center of American politics sharply to the right.

A late friend was a rather well-known political scientist who specialized in studying political extremism in the United States. He studied communists on the left, fascists on the right, and variations at each extreme. Now, he would have difficulty justifying such a specialty. A study of extremism, almost by definition, is a study of the fringe. Now, contrary to the situation on the left, with a few exceptions there is little difference between what once was fringe of the right, and the Republican Party. The extreme has become normalized. What studying the far right was in the days before Reagan, now for the most part is simply studying American politics. Much of the dangerous white nationalist movement has now been absorbed. When "good people on both sides" became normalized, most of the far right had ceased to be on the fringe. It had its representative in the presidential chair, and his cabal of advisers and cabinet-level enablers.

There is virtually no hard left in American politics; certainly nothing of significance. Communism, never appealing to large numbers, has almost no adherents. Democratic socialists here advocate policies that in much of the world would be seen as simply centrist, common sense. For the most part, "leftists" in this country are not far left at all. Bernie Sanders in most countries would be a thoughtful centrist. As for studying the far right, such as members of the old John Birch Society, most of the extremist ideas they professed are little different from those of most of today's Republicans.

The movement that led to a more ideological judiciary (and it certainly still contains many exceptions) was not one that any president initiated exclusively, although both Richard Nixon and Ronald Reagan contributed. As I have discussed elsewhere, citing Michael Kruse, the growing conservative movement influenced a weekend conference at Yale that led to an upending of American politics.

Reagan's election inspired a group of Yale conservatives who brought together a large group of 200 or so, on a weekend in April of 1982. I was nowhere near New England, but can attest to near-fanatic enthusiasm among conservatives at the time, excited by Reagan's presidency, in the Midwest and the Southwest. I'm sure that similar expressions of zealotry could have been found almost everywhere in the country. For example, I remember a party in the Midwest, in early 1980, when an oh-so-earnest young woman, the wife of an ultra-conservative congressional staffer, implored me to sign a petition for Reagan to be the Republican nominee. Considering her situation, she should have known that presidential nominations don't result from petitions, nor would I be likely to sign one in any event. Nevertheless, she said, breathlessly, that, please, she wanted my input—my total input. She received not even my partial input, although I was polite ...

The Yale group included government officials, judges, prominent conservative writers, and legal scholars. Ordinarily, such groupings generate excitement, some articles, and little else. This one led to the formation of the Federalist Society. It would be difficult, likely impossible, to identify any other group that ultimately has had such influence. However much the Federalist Society professes to be a non-partisan debating group, Kruse points out that it was enormously aggressive from the beginning, "steeling for a fight," as he put it in a revealing article, "The Weekend at Yale that Changed American Politics" (*Politico*, January 18, 2018). Among those present were Robert Bork, and Antonin Scalia, before Reagan put him on the Court.

The Society for years has encouraged bright young conservatives to study law, become lawyers, and especially to become judges. As could have been expected, conservative billionaires, such as the Kochs, have lavished funds to assist. The Federalist Society has been one of the most influential groups in American political history. It not only has contributed to changing the character of the judiciary but encouraged the conservative takeover of American politics.

The very success of the conservatives has led to enormous excess. Tax changes beginning with Reagan have led to huge income disparities and have made possible what once was an impossibility: multi-billionaires. That excess finally, beginning in the off-year elections of 2018, led to such a reaction that it can only be called a revolution: a blue revolution. This is one that elected a centrist, Joe Biden along with Kamala Harris, and created the conditions that led the new president to the culmination of his long political journey on the road to becoming— what once would have seemed quite far-fetched—a great progressive reformer.

From Reagan onward, Republicans have packed the courts with Federalist Society members, while Democrats generally have tried to avoid controversy by picking moderates. There is no doubt that conservatives tend as a rule to be the most confrontational, I must say, nasty, people in American politics. Yes, there are exceptions on both sides, but liberals and moderates tend to be more "reasonable," and seek to understand the viewpoints of others. Conservatives almost to a person, couldn't care less what others think, so long as they win. Democratic presidents have tended to consult with members of both parties in selecting nominees; conservatives do all they can to ram through rightist ideologues.

I must mention something ironic, though. As I remarked back at the beginning, Steven Calabresi, a co-founder of that very Federalist Society, extreme or not, has retained his principles.

Calabresi was so outraged at the president's rant suggesting that he might postpone the election, that he said it was "fascistic." That alone was enough, he said, for the president to be impeached again, and to be quickly removed from office. Within weeks, the voters had done the job of removal themselves.

Contemporary Republican ideas of consultation are: "my way or the highway, and the hell with you," McConnell is notorious for the stolen seat, rationalizing it by saying it had become traditional not to confirm a justice late in a president's term. He was lying, of course. Justice Kennedy was sitting on the Court when McConnell pulled his stunt, and McConnell and many other Republicans had been in the Senate when it confirmed Kennedy. The Senate confirmed Kennedy, a Reagan nominee, in Reagan's last year in office. McConnell voted to confirm him, as did the entire Senate—and it was a Senate controlled by Democrats who were confirming a Republican president's nominee. Later, McConnell admitted, rather bragged, that if a Republican president nominates a justice in the last year of his time in office, Republicans would confirm. Of course they would, as they demonstrated by moving quickly to begin the process of filling Justice Ginsburg's seat as soon as they learned of her death.

The Republican miscreants denied President Obama his constitutionally-mandated authority to fill a vacancy when they succeeded in stealing a seat on the Court. The Senate was not obligated to confirm an Obama nomination, of course, but in refusing even to consider his nomination of Merrick Garland, the Republican senators were ignoring a duly-elected president's authority to submit a nomination. That demonstrated a rude disrespect for Barack Obama, and also disrespect for the institution of the presidency. Comparing their performance then with their zeal to fill the Ginsburg vacancy put their hypocrisy on vivid display for the amazement of the world.

The Court occasionally issues a decision that departs from its general hard-right orientation. That is not sufficient, however. The record of the contemporary Court reflects hostility to voting rights and the rights of minorities. Consider *Bush v. Gore* in 2000 that forced a halt to Florida's recount and handed the presidency to the Republican, George W. Bush, who lost the popular vote. In 2010, the *Citizens United* decision proclaimed political spending to be a form of free speech, which certainly granted far more speech to wealthy interests than to others. This was directly anti-democratic, class based, and protected the political "rights" of corporations in contrast to those of actual voters. It caused, as critics forecast, an absolute flood of money, even more than before, into politics. In 2013, *Shelby v. Holder* gutted a key provision of the Voting Rights Act that had protected voters of color against suppression since 1965. The assumption was that racial bias no longer existed. In 2019, the *Rucho* decision declared that it was perfectly acceptable to gerrymander to benefit one political party over another (remember North Carolina, with a majority of the vote for Democrats, but a victory for 10 out of 13 congressional seats for Republicans?). These decisions were 5 to 4, and these were only the most notorious.

Even in other decisions, there were troublesome elements. In another 5 to 4 decision in 2012 that upheld the Affordable Care Act (*National Federation of Independent Business v Sebelius*), the Court struck down the right of Congress to compel states to expand Medicaid. Twelve states still deny their poor citizens health coverage, even though the federal government pays 90% of the cost of expansion and pours vast sums of needed money into the states. That decision raised questions about the application of the Commerce Clause that is the basis for most of the federal economic activity since the New Deal. That is a potential time bomb.

The great Democratic victories in 2020 made it possible to correct much of the damage. The damage had been years in the making, though, and may be stubborn, requiring long, continued, efforts to redress. Things do seem to be proceeding rapidly, but obstacles may yet arise. Once in office, President Biden moved quickly to expand the Court. Considering the Republicans' conduct, this should have been anticipated. At one time, this would have been shocking, but numerous Democrats and liberal writers—even including the thoughtful Michelle Goldberg of the New York Times—had concluded that it had become essential. Biden agreed, and moved to add four seats, to compensate for improper appointments and to keep the membership at an odd number." He is just now preparing to sign the legislation that will bring the membership to thirteen. Some liberals agree with the need for reform, but caution against "packing." In response, I point out that the damage has been severe, and has been consistent and systematic over decades. Drastic action must immediately provide some correction. The need is urgent but does not preclude structural reform later.

This expansion adds one member to compensate for the first recent Republican appointee, who took the seat that Moscow Mitch had stolen, and another to compensate for the second appointee, Brett Kavanaugh, who was unqualified on grounds of judicial temperament, but was confirmed nonetheless. Kavanaugh demonstrated openly to the country that he undoubtedly lacked the maturity and the judicial temperament required for an effective Justice of the Supreme Court. The "moderate" Senator Susan Collins should have been ashamed to cast her vote that assured his confirmation, but she expressed confidence that he would be objective. Happily, her own performances in purporting to be a moderate led to her crushing defeat in 2020, along with those of her Republican fellows and her president. She drowned, politically, in the blue tsunami; deservedly so.

No more "Lucy and the football" farces from her will corrupt America's policies.

President Biden, as he prepared to sign this legislation, has kept his counsel and not commented on the nominations. The assumption is prevalent, though, and I think is correct, that for at least two of these positions he will name African-American women. I applaud, and say it's past time for such appointments. Biden is not perfect, as he (in contrast to his predecessor) concedes; in his long career, he has made numerous missteps, which he also admits. Most relevant here (although he has served as Chair of the powerful Senate Committee on Foreign Relations, and clearly believes in diplomacy and allies), he served for some eight years as Chair of the Senate Judiciary Committee, and certainly will choose superb candidates, as he did for his vice president. There is no question that the overwhelmingly Democratic majority in the Senate will confirm them all speedily, no doubt breathing sighs of relief as they do so. They have the votes to quash any filibuster.

As for the filibuster, Democrats now have the will, should the need ever present itself, to abolish the generally loathsome practice entirely. People forget that filibusters did not always exist, nor that when they emerged, their function was almost always to cater to the racist demands of the south and continue the oppression of America's Black citizens. Most arguments defending the filibuster, although phrased in the language of protecting the minority, cannot disguise its undemocratic function. That is, instead of honoring each member's vote, the filibuster permits a privileged minority to thwart majority will. Occasionally, that is justified, but overwhelmingly it operates to permit an elite minority to repress majority wishes for reform. The Senate's arcane rules even permit a single senator, at times, to block the majority. Republican Senator Rand Paul, for example, continued the long-standing tradition of southern bigots by blocking a bill against lynching.

As for President Biden's Court nominations, it would be a welcome culmination if they could include Anita Hill, whom he treated poorly during the hearings for Justice Clarence Thomas in 1991. Joe Biden, although flawed, is a good, and decent, man—quite unlike his immediate predecessor. He has grown considerably since then, and while more growth is in order, he continues to demonstrate development as president, as with his selection of Kamala Harris as vice president; sometimes astonishingly so. Nevertheless of course it would be unrealistic to expect such a delightful, and delightfully ironic, appointment of a Justice Anita Hill. Regardless, Hill should be honored for her valiant efforts long ago, and for the wounds she suffered.

This Court's record made it necessary for the victorious Democrats to take extreme measures to restore balance to the judiciary. This is not to seek revenge. That may be satisfying, but it is not productive in the long run, and does not work toward the country's good. Rather, the US needs a competent judiciary that is reasonable, and that operates to uphold the law and the Constitution, interpreted reasonably according to existing conditions.

The Court soon will proceed with its 13 members, and its new progressive majority. For the long run, though, President Biden has appointed a study group to recommend revisions to the entire federal judiciary. The group recently issued a preliminary report speculating on possible revisions. Of course it recommends legislation providing specifically that spending money is not "speech," and that corporations are not "persons," with rights. Some conservatives say that such a denial of corporate "free speech" would open, say, the *New York Times* to repressive censorship. Nonsense. Perhaps it would if there were no First Amendment, but the Constitution explicitly protects freedom of the press, and it does not have to resort to calling corporations people to do so. If the "corporate free speech" advocates were consistent, they would have to oppose corporations purchasing one another. The Thirteenth Amendment makes it plain that persons cannot own each other. It seems unlikely that any businessperson would push the notion of corporate personhood that far.

From the beginning, the court structure at the federal level has had three tiers, district courts for the lowest courts of record, with each state entitled at least to one. The highest court is the one the Constitution itself established, the U. S. Supreme Court. In between, there has always been an appellate function.

When President Grant signed the Judiciary Act of 1869, he authorized the beginnings of permanent judicial appointments to hear appeals in each judicial circuit. For the first time, each circuit had a permanent judge to preside (unless a justice from the Supreme Court were "riding circuit" and were present) when considering appeals. Grant was scrupulous in nominating the new appeals judges to ensure that the circuits would be vigorous in enforcing the new Civil War Amendments.

The Judiciary Act of 1891, signed by President Benjamin Harrison, the Evarts Act, created the U. S. Courts of Appeals. Each judicial circuit would have a formal Circuit Court established, with another permanent judge who would preside. That judge, the existing appeals court judge, and a district judge would hear appeals from district courts, and would constitute the new, three-judge, court. Those courts have grown in size through the years.

Thus, there has been variation through the years regarding the structure of the appeals function. The study group is suggesting that a new structure should be considered. It would create a parallel court for each existing US Circuit Court, and a new

National Court of Constitutional Appeals. The new courts in the circuits would consider appeals from district courts dealing with civil liberties and constitutional issues. The National Court would hear appeals from the circuits that dealt with those issues. Its decisions would be final. The appellate function of the U.S. Supreme Court therefore would be reduced, and there would be no appeal from the National Court to the Supreme Court.

The new structure, newly staffed, would serve to add balance to the federal judiciary, that had been largely skewed toward the ideological by decades of Republican ideological rigidity. All this could be done with no constitutional amendment, since the Congress has the authority to create new courts, and also the authority to regulate the appellate jurisdiction of the Supreme Court. The Report also suggests that the new National Court be much larger than the Supreme Court, that smaller groups of its judges would hear cases with the possibility of appealing to the full National Court, functioning as circuit courts do today. This would put less attention on that court, helping perhaps to reduce its politicization, and would place considerably less attention on each appointment to that court, so that they would not carry the political baggage that contemporary appointments do. With constitutional and civil liberties issues taken from the Supreme Court, that court also would be in a position to become less politicized as the years pass.

End of Material from the Journal

CHAPTER 9

HATE IN THE TIME OF CORONAVIRUS

That completes the material from my journal, and I hope that you, your children, and others find it instructive. Before closing, I think I should provide some additional comments on how we came to go through such dysfunctional politics, and what we might expect for the future.

Of course, we need to go about our lives, and try to recapture some semblance of normality, but also, we need to improve the normal, far beyond what it had been. This is possible, as these early months of the Biden presidency have demonstrated so clearly. If we are to retain the improvements we have seen already, though, it's essential to advance and not be static. For the good of ourselves, and for everyone else, this must be our future.

Of course, we cannot be expected to concentrate fully on reform, either as individual citizens, or as a government. We have our own lives to live. We have nothing if we can't have fulfilling lives, but we are responsible for doing what we can so that others can have them also. A little bit of Thoreau is suggestive here.

Where Do We Go From Here?

When going for reform keep things in perspective. For example, this may be surprising, but in my view, we need a strong president, and a strong presidency. Our system works better when the executive is strong and vigorous, and it is only when there is leadership from the center, that progressive reform is possible. There have been too few progressive periods in American history. When the time is right for progressive reform, such as now, a strong president is essential to take advantage of the opportunities.

Of course, a strong presidency can be dangerous, so it must operate within strict limits. To be effective, rather than dangerous, the president needs to be vigorous, but respect the roles of other branches and respect the roles of the presidency itself. Biden's predecessor had no such respect, and knew too little to have any idea about what that involved. He knew nothing about how presidents must act in our system, and did not care. He operated by whim, and tweet, burning, tearing down, and destroying with abandon. His idea of a legacy was to have his name and face remembered, not to make the system function better. Sadly, his party followed his corrupted example. In the 2020 election, it did not even bother to produce a platform. Its formal plan was simply to follow its president's lead—apparently without regard to direction, or extent.

Basic competence must be a prerequisite for public officials. Unfortunately, that cannot be considered as a given. As we have just witnessed, candidate selection is vital, as is the method of choosing the winner. That presupposes elimination of the electoral college. The dangers it presents now should be obvious, and cannot be overstated.

Some basic principles must be incorporated into the system. People have rights. Corporations are business groupings, they have their place, but are not people. Spending money is not speech and must never be protected by government as though it is part of the Bill of Rights. Citizens have the same rights equally as it pertains to speech; some do not legally have vastly more right to speak than others. If money truly were speech, some people, by definition, would have far more right to speak than others. That offends every principle of democracy, as does the power of a rogue executive to pardon miscreants who have participated with him in law breaking, thus protecting henchmen. The principle that no one should be the judge when affected personally should certainly govern with regard to the pardon power.

Similarly, governments exercise the authority appropriate for governments. They must not delegate that authority to private corporations. Prisons, for better or worse, are government entities. Obviously, the entire enterprise needs to be re-thought, and reformed. Neither private prisons nor other private enterprises should ever exist to exercise powers—especially powers over citizens—that legitimately belong only to government. And obviously, the government's authority should never be delegated to private groups for profit.

As for the two-party system, the 2020 victory was so overwhelming, that a sea change may be in order. After the Goldwater debacle of 1964, there were predictions that the Republican Party was so wounded that it was no longer viable. Four years later, that Party had so recovered, that Republicans elected Richard Nixon, narrowly, to be sure. Four years after that, though, Nixon won re-election in one of the greatest popular-vote landslides in American political history. Roughly two years after that, Nixon was forced from office in disgrace, although his transgressions, serious as they were, outrageous as they were, were nothing compared to the recently-defeated Republican.

Thus, nothing is certain. The magnitude of this recent defeat, however, and the damage to the reputation of the Republican Party, far exceed anything before. The misdeeds include everything up to, and even including, treason. There is good reason to think that the party may vanish, as well it should.

We are told by reformers, that we need a new, and responsible, conservative party to replace the Republicans. That would certainly be an improvement, but considering the magnitude of "conservatism's" failures, it seems more reasonable that the existing Democratic Party may grow, with its most progressive wing splitting off, therefore leaving a centrist, and a center-left, party; a new two-party system, with each party offering reasonable policies, and an ability to work together, to compromise, and to return American politics to a more smoothly-functioning basis, offering alternatives on both sides that work. This would abandon the rightist policies—austerity, small-government, and the like—that over and over demonstrate their unworkability and that impose hardship upon the people.

Better Understanding of How Things Deteriorated So Badly

Traditionally, American politicians of nearly all varieties worked together for the good of the country. They had extreme disagreements on how that was to be done, but when a policy became law, they did their best to make it function as well as it could, and to improve it regularly. Medicare and civil rights are good examples. Conservatives opposed them vigorously, but when passage became inevitable under LBJ, many cooperated with the administration to craft the laws, and make them work. At the extreme, there might be attempts to change or repeal the law. Never did they seek to make a law fail in order to cause maximum damage to their opponents by harming the country, as Republicans tried persistently to do to the Affordable Care Act until their recent defeat. Before the Gingrich-engineered political death struggles, bitter controversies on the floor of the House or Senate could flourish, with all sides seeking to advance their positions, but animosity typically halted as legislators left the chamber. They socialized. Political enemies often were personal friends.

Newt Gingrich produced a halt to all that. Opponents were not mere policy adversaries, they were the enemy, and had to be destroyed, not only politically but personally as well. For purposes of immediate political gain, he worked to develop disrespect for Congress as an institution. This, no doubt unwittingly, seemed to pave the way for the potential destruction of the United States as a democratic republic. That culminated in the administration of the last Republican president, who astonished not only Americans, but the entire world with his complete unsuitability for the job.

How was it that so many normal Americans could have been taken in by a presidential candidate who violated the norms of acceptable behavior, consistently failed at business, was manifestly cruel, selfish, and abusive, and lied constantly? Even his constant boasting violated one of the basic rules of civilized humanity: don't brag. Yet he recognized no restraint, arguing that he was infallible, uniquely talented, able easily to accomplish the seemingly impossible, and claiming to have done so even after stark failure. Claiming to be mistreated because he had not been awarded a Nobel Peace Prize or had not been chosen to have his face on Mount Rushmore, should almost be a guarantee always of severe mental imbalance, but his base overlooked it all.

Part of the explanation, of course, is that many of those on the right had developed such hatred of liberals, "libtard cucks and snowflakes," that they concluded anything that might upset their objects of scorn was worth any price. That not only is irrational but is a sad principle to adopt as fundamental to one's politics. I continue to be amazed at their tolerance for a president who personally violated nearly all their prejudices. They unquestionably responded to his rhetoric, rather than to his actions. They seemed enthralled by his belligerence. Oddly, their tolerance of him did not carry over to his appointees, however delighted they were at first when two extreme conservatives received their seats on the Supreme Court.

Their uneasiness with the performance of his judicial appointments also had little or no effect on their opinion of the president who made the nominations. It is simple to discern the truth of the theme that I wove through one of my recent books,

Unworkable Conservatism: The principles that modern Americans who call themselves "conservative" advocate are extremely difficult to put into practice. In the rare instances when they are implemented, they satisfy no one, including their most fervent adherents.

Yet their conclusion is not that their principles are impractical. Rather, they convince themselves—forgetting the law of holes; when in one, if you want to get out, stop digging—that their "conservative" principles failed only because they were not conservative enough.

The new conservative ideologues on the Supreme Court failed to meet their expectation (on the rare occasions when one of their rulings evoked displeasure) because they were not "really" conservative. A "real conservative" has to be pure; devotion to the cause can admit of no exceptions and every action must be shaped by extremist ideology.

And so it goes. Rational argument, reasoned persuasion, went nowhere.

There are no doubt many reasons for this. Confirmation bias, the tendency of any new information to strengthen one's previous conviction, of course was in play. George Lakoff brought linguistics to bear when he demonstrated the extent to which persuasion depended upon the manner in which an issue was "framed," despite its content. Drew Westin, similarly, employed social psychology to illustrate how much persuasion in order to be effective required appeals to emotion, rather than to reason.

I believe, though, there was another strong factor. Many Bible colleges did, and do, teach what they call "harmonization." Because they insist on biblical inerrancy, they believe that every word in the Bible is, and must be, literally true and that therefore the Bible can contain no contradiction. This insistence creates difficulties for them, because with its numerous authors and sometimes vague implications The Bible presents many contradictions. The discerning reader will immediately be struck in early Genesis that in one presentation God creates whales, etc., and then creates Adam, while in another, adjacent one, God creates Adam, and then, sensing his loneliness, creates other animals and finally, Eve.

In dealing with such inconsistencies, many evangelicals teach mental techniques that "harmonize" the inconsistencies that "really only seem to exist because the human mind is incapable of fully understanding God's truth." As though they were dealing with impossible mental exercises such as Zen koans, for example, the "sound of one hand clapping," they meditate on the apparent contradiction until they can rationalize it away, and accept that Adam and other animals each can have been created before the other, and make themselves believe that irreconcilable statements can both be correct.

It is common today to see politicians and others who reject science, and even the notion of truth. Tyrants certainly benefit from a gullible population that overlooks, or "harmonizes" away any conflict between the flawed character of a leader and the professed advantages of continuing to support, even revere, that person despite—or even because of—the manifest defects displayed.

The fundamentalist approach to Christianity became so pervasive in American politics that it makes sense to wonder whether the widespread ability to reject logic and fact in religion may also have caused people accustomed to thinking in such a manner to approach politics, economics, and social matters in the same way by rejecting reality.

This, of course, is simply speculation on my part. Whether or not such far-reaching fundamentalist practice is one of the dynamics at work, another that is directly hostile to American interests, and is explicitly political, definitely was and is in play. That is the myth, certainly generated by propaganda from Russian intelligence, that the heart of true Christianity today is to be found in Russia.

You know, certainly, that I am not presenting a scholarly study here, or a research report. Now and then, though, I may supply some documentation, just in case something may seem doubtful. Consider voices from the world of theology.

Christianity Today published an article (July/August 2018) by Jayson Casper, titled, "Mideast Christians See Russia—Not the U.S.—as Defender of their Faith."[1] He noted that it remains unclear whether the relationship is more than political expediency, but there is no doubt that it exists.

Journals outside the realm of theology also have picked up the same theme.

Max Seddon, writing in *Financial Times* ("Putin and the Patriarchs," August 21, 2019), describes Putin's effort reaching out to Christians to "highlight divisions between Russia and the supposedly amoral west, and to elevate the idea of the 'Russian world,' a sort of spiritual dominion." *Think Progress* (June 19, 2018) describes "plotting" between Russians and the American right that began as early as 1995. It quotes notes from "the first meeting," and says that this plotting influenced America's home-schooling movement.[2] Tom Porter in *Newsweek,* (Sep-

---

1   A theologian at Pittsburgh Theological Seminary, Jon Burgess, published an online article (August 2, 2018) for the same journal, on "The Unexpected Relationship Between U.S. Evangelicals and Russian Orthodox." https://www.christiancentury.org/article/features/unexpected-relationship-between-us-evangelicals-and-russian-orthodox.

2   https://archive.thinkprogress.org/americas-biggest-right-wing-home-schooling-group-has-been-networking-with-sanctioned-russians-1f2b5b5ad031/

tember 15, 2018), said "The Christian Right is Looking to Putin's Russia to Save Christianity from the Godless West."

Despite some strains, Putin has gained control of Russian espionage, and also has gained substantial influence within the Russian Orthodox Church. He shrewdly, and successfully, has groomed American fundamentalist-evangelical leaders to become allies of the Putin-dominated religion, just as he groomed the former president to become his ally politically, years ago when the future president was only a real-estate developer preoccupied with swindling the unwary.

This helps to explain why American conservatives in general, and American fundamentalist-evangelicals in particular, tread regularly up to the boundaries of treason, and often don't hesitate to step—or leap—beyond. Considering the heritage of strong, even frantic, anti-communism, and anti-Soviet (hence, anti-Russian) sentiments traditional among the American right, it is more than ironic that apologies for Russian Putin-style tyranny and sympathy for Putin the strong man became characteristic of the far right in America. Viewing contemporary right-wing politics in the United States reveals its adherents to be faux patriots who have no patience with traditional American principles of liberty and individual worth.

The irony, the tragedy, of the American right is that the two strains it manifests, and has made pervasive in American politics, are both products of some of history's greatest losers. Despite the right's pious rhetoric of patriotic values, and chest-thumping Americanism, both these strains are explicitly contrary to the values that America officially has always professed as its fundamental rationale: individual liberty, and consent of the governed.

The first great loser is the secessionist Confederacy that failed in its attempt to destroy the United States. This reflects the heritage of the old south in America: human chattel slavery with its legacy of racism and property rights that suppress individual liberty. The second great loser is the old Soviet Union. That late superpower has left a legacy from totalitarian communism, with Putin, who channels the tyranny of the old KGB through the modern Russian state and through the contemporary Russian Orthodox Church.

These forces seduced gullible American "conservatives," especially fundamental-evangelicals, and other followers of America's corrupt 45th president, who gleefully submitted while he subordinated the values of his—and their—country to those of foreign dictators. Their support continued in spite of this president's open preference for foreign authoritarianism; or perhaps actually *because* of it.

We now have an opportunity to make things whole again. There is reason to be optimistic. The disgraced president did have one significant accomplishment. He made us open to rational reform and seems to have succeeded in destroying the Republican Party after it had misbehaved for decades. One can hope.

Here it is, the summary: one time, and one time only, never to be repeated:

Trump: Loser!